Fanshawe

Fanshawe

NATHANIEL HAWTHORNE

Serenity
Publishers, LLC

ROCKVILLE, MARYLAND
2009

ISBN: 978-1-60450-553-5

Published by Serenity Publishers
An Arc Manor Company
P. O. Box 10339
Rockville, MD 20849-0339
www.SerenityPublishers.com
Printed in the United States of America/United Kingdom

INTRODUCTORY NOTE

IN 1828, three years after graduating from Bowdoin College, Hawthorne published his first romance, "Fanshawe." It was issued at Boston by Marsh & Capen, but made little or no impression on the public. The motto on the title-page of the original was from Southey: "Wilt thou go on with me?"

Afterwards, when he had struck into the vein of fiction that came to be known as distinctively his own, he attempted to suppress this youthful work, and was so successful that he obtained and destroyed all but a few of the copies then extant.

Some twelve years after his death it was resolved, in view of the interest manifested in tracing the growth of his genius from the beginning of his activity as an author, to revive this youthful romance; and the reissue of "Fanshawe" was then made.

Little biographical interest attaches to it, beyond the fact that Mr. Longfellow found in the descriptions and general atmosphere of the book a decided suggestion of the situation of Bowdoin College, at Brunswick, Maine, and the life there at the time when he and Hawthorne were both undergraduates of that institution.

Professor Packard, of Bowdoin College, who was then in charge of the study of English literature, and has survived both of his illustrious pupils, recalls Hawthorne's exceptional excellence in the composition of English, even at that date (1821-1825); and it is not impossible that Hawthorne intended, through the character of Fanshawe, to present some faint projection of what he then thought might be his own obscure history. Even while he was in college, however, and meditating perhaps the slender elements of this first romance, his fellow-student Horatio Bridge, whose "Journal of an African Cruiser" he afterwards edited, recognized in him the possibilities of a writer of fiction—a fact to which Hawthorne alludes in the dedicatory Preface to "The Snow-Image."

G. P. L.

CHAPTER I

"Our court shall be a little Academe."

SHAKESPEARE.

IN an ancient though not very populous settlement, in a retired corner of one of the New England States, arise the walls of a seminary of learning, which, for the convenience of a name, shall be entitled "Harley College." This institution, though the number of its years is inconsiderable compared with the hoar antiquity of its European sisters, is not without some claims to reverence on the score of age; for an almost countless multitude of rivals, by many of which its reputation has been eclipsed, have sprung up since its foundation. At no time, indeed, during an existence of nearly a century, has it acquired a very extensive fame; and circumstances, which need not be particularized, have, of late years, involved it in a deeper obscurity. There are now few candidates for the degrees that the college is authorized to bestow. On two of its annual "Commencement Days," there has been a total deficiency of baccalaureates; and the lawyers and divines, on whom doctorates in their respective professions are gratuitously inflicted, are not accustomed to consider the distinction as an honor. Yet the sons of this seminary have always maintained their full share of reputation, in whatever paths of life they trod. Few of them, perhaps, have been deep and finished scholars; but the college has supplied—what the emergencies of the country demanded—a set of men more useful in its present state, and whose deficiency in theoretical knowledge has not been found to imply a want of practical ability.

The local situation of the college, so far secluded from the sight and sound of the busy world, is peculiarly favorable to the moral, if not to the literary, habits of its students; and this advantage probably caused the founders to overlook the inconveniences that were inseparably connected with it. The humble edifices rear themselves almost at the farthest extremity of a narrow vale, which, winding through a long extent of hill-country, is wellnigh as inaccessible, except at one point, as the Happy Valley of Abyssinia. A stream, that farther on becomes a considerable river, takes its rise at, a short distance above the college, and affords, along its wood-fringed banks, many shady retreats, where even study is pleasant, and idleness delicious. The neighborhood of the institution is not quite a solitude, though the few habitations scarcely constitute a village. These consist principally of farm-houses, of rather an ancient date (for the settlement is much older than the college), and of a little inn, which even in that secluded spot does not fail of a moderate support. Other dwellings are scattered up and down the valley; but the difficulties of the soil will long avert the evils of a too dense population. The character of the inhabitants does not seem—as there was, perhaps, room to anticipate—to be in any degree influenced by the atmosphere of Harley College. They are a set of rough and hardy yeomen, much inferior, as respects refinement, to the corresponding classes in most other parts of our country. This is the more remarkable, as there is scarcely a family in the vicinity that has not provided, for at least one of its sons, the advantages of a "liberal education."

Having thus described the present state of Harley College, we must proceed to speak of it as it existed about eighty years since, when its foundation was recent, and its prospects flattering. At the head of the institution, at this period, was a learned and Orthodox divine, whose fame was in all the churches. He was the author of several works which evinced much erudition and depth of research; and the public, perhaps, thought the more highly of his abilities from a singularity in the purposes to which he applied them, that added much to the curiosity of his labors, though little to their usefulness. But, however fanciful might be his private pursuits, Dr. Melmoth, it was universally allowed, was diligent and successful in the arts of instruction. The young men of his charge prospered beneath his eye, and regarded him with an affection that was strengthened by the little foibles which occasionally excited their ridicule. The president was assisted in the discharge of his duties by two inferior officers, chosen from the alumni of the college, who, while they imparted to others the knowledge they had already imbibed, pursued the study of divinity under the direction of their principal. Under such auspices the institution grew and flourished. Having at that time but two rivals in the country (neither of them within a considerable distance), it became the general resort of the youth of the Province in which it was situated. For several years in succession, its students amounted to nearly fifty,—a number which, relatively to the circumstances of the country, was very considerable.

From the exterior of the collegians, an accurate observer might pretty safely judge how long they had been inmates of those classic walls. The brown cheeks and the rustic dress of some would inform him that they had but recently left the plough to labor in a not less toilsome field; the grave look, and the intermingling of garments of a more classic cut, would distinguish those who had begun to acquire the polish of their new residence; and the air of superiority, the paler cheek, the less robust form, the spectacles of green, and the dress, in general of threadbare black, would designate the highest class, who were understood to have acquired nearly all the science their Alma Mater could bestow, and to be on the point of assuming their stations in the world. There were, it is true, exceptions to this general description. A few young men had found their way hither from the distant seaports; and these were the models of fashion to their rustic companions, over whom they asserted a superiority in exterior accomplishments, which the fresh though unpolished intellect of the sons of the forest denied them in their literary competitions. A third class, differing widely from both the former, consisted of a few young descendants of the aborigines, to whom an impracticable philanthropy was endeavoring to impart the benefits of civilization.

If this institution did not offer all the advantages of elder and prouder seminaries, its deficiencies were compensated to its students by the inculcation of regular habits, and of a deep and awful sense of religion, which seldom deserted them in their course through life. The mild and gentle rule of Dr. Melmoth, like that of a father over his children, was more destructive to vice than a sterner sway; and though youth is never without its follies, they have seldom been more harmless than they were here. The students, indeed, ignorant of their own bliss, sometimes wished to hasten the time of their entrance on the business of life; but they found, in after-years, that many of their happiest remembrances, many of the scenes which they would with least reluctance live over again, referred to the seat of their early studies. The exceptions to this remark were chiefly those whose vices had drawn down, even from that paternal government, a weighty retribution.

Dr. Melmoth, at the time when he is to be introduced to the reader, had borne the matrimonial yoke (and in his case it was no light burden) nearly twenty years. The blessing of children, however, had been denied him,—a circumstance which he was accustomed to consider as one of the sorest trials that checkered his pathway; for he was a man of a kind and affectionate heart, that was continually seeking objects to rest itself upon. He was inclined to believe, also, that a common offspring would have exerted a meliorating influence on the temper of Mrs. Melmoth, the character of whose domestic government often compelled him to call to mind such portions of the wisdom of antiquity as relate to the proper endurance of the shrewishness of woman. But domestic comforts, as well as comforts of every other kind, have their drawbacks; and, so long as the balance is on the side of happiness, a wise man will not murmur. Such was the opinion of Dr. Melmoth; and with a little aid from philosophy, and more from religion, he journeyed on contentedly through life. When the storm was loud by the parlor hearth, he had always a sure and quiet retreat in his study; and there, in his deep though not always useful labors, he soon forgot whatever of disagreeable nature pertained to his situation. This small and dark apartment was the only portion of the house to which, since one firmly repelled invasion, Mrs. Melmoth's omnipotence did not extend. Here (to reverse the words of Queen Elizabeth) there was "but one master and no mistress"; and that man has little right to complain who possesses so much as one corner in the world where he may be happy or miserable, as best suits him. In his study, then, the doctor was accustomed to spend most of the hours that were unoccupied by the duties of his station. The flight of time was here as swift as the wind, and noiseless as the snowflake; and it was a sure proof of real happiness that night often came upon the student before he knew it was midday.

Dr. Melmoth was wearing towards age (having lived nearly sixty years), when he was called upon to assume a character to which he had as yet been a stranger. He had possessed in his youth a very dear friend, with whom his education had associated him, and who in his early manhood had been his chief intimate. Circumstances, however, had separated them for nearly thirty years, half of which had been spent by his friend, who was engaged in mercantile pursuits, in a foreign country. The doctor had, nevertheless, retained a warm interest in the welfare of his old associate, though the different nature of their thoughts and occupations had prevented them from corresponding. After a silence of so long continuance, therefore, he was surprised by the receipt of a letter from his friend, containing a request of a most unexpected nature.

Mr. Langton had married rather late in life; and his wedded bliss had been but of short continuance. Certain misfortunes in trade, when he was a Benedict of three years' standing, had deprived him of a large portion of his property, and compelled him, in order to save the remainder, to leave his own country for what he hoped would be but a brief residence in another. But, though he was successful in the immediate objects of his voyage, circumstances occurred to lengthen his stay far beyond the period which he had assigned to it. It was difficult so to arrange his extensive concerns that they could be safely trusted to the management of others; and, when this was effected, there was another not less powerful obstacle to his return. His affairs, under his own inspection, were so prosperous, and his gains so considerable, that, in the words of the old ballad, "He set his heart to gather gold"; and to this absorbing passion he sacrificed his domestic happiness. The death of his wife, about four years after his departure, undoubtedly contributed to give him a sort of dread of returning, which it required a strong effort to overcome. The welfare of his only child he knew would be little affected by this event; for she was under the protection of his sister, of whose tenderness he was well assured. But, after a few more years, this sister, also, was taken away by death; and then the father felt that duty imperatively called upon him to return. He realized, on a sudden, how much of life he had thrown away in the acquisition of what is only valuable as it contributes to the happiness of life, and how short a tune was left him for life's true enjoyments. Still, however, his mercantile habits were too deeply seated to allow him to hazard his present prosperity by any hasty measures; nor was Mr. Langton, though capable of strong affections, naturally liable to manifest them violently. It was probable, therefore, that many months might yet elapse before he would again tread the shores of his native country.

But the distant relative, in whose family, since the death of her aunt, Ellen Langton had remained, had been long at variance with her father, and had unwillingly assumed the office of her protector. Mr. Langton's request, therefore, to Dr. Melmoth, was, that his ancient friend (one of the few friends that time had left him) would be as a father to his daughter till he could himself relieve him of the charge.

The doctor, after perusing the epistle of his friend, lost no time in laying it before Mrs. Melmoth, though this was, in truth, one of the very few occasions on which he had determined that his will should be absolute law. The lady was quick to perceive the firmness of his purpose, and would not (even had she been particularly averse to the proposed measure) hazard her usual authority by a fruitless opposition. But, by long disuse, she had lost the power of consenting graciously to any wish of her husband's.

"I see your heart is set upon this matter," she observed; "and, in truth, I fear we cannot decently refuse Mr. Langton's request. I see little good of such a friend, doctor, who never lets one know he is alive till he has a favor to ask."

"Nay; but I have received much good at his hand," replied Dr. Melmoth; "and, if he asked more of me, it should be done with a willing heart. I remember in my youth, when my worldly goods were few and ill managed (I was a bachelor, then, dearest Sarah, with none to look after my household), how many times I have been beholden to him. And see—in his letter he speaks of presents, of the produce of the country, which he has sent both to you and me."

"If the girl were country-bred," continued the lady, "we might give her house-room, and no harm done. Nay, she might even be a help to me; for Esther, our maid-servant, leaves us at the mouth's end. But I warrant she knows as little of household matters as you do yourself, doctor."

"My friend's sister was well grounded in the *re familiari*" answered her husband; "and doubtless she hath imparted somewhat of her skill to this damsel. Besides, the child is of tender years, and will profit much by your instruction and mine."

"The child is eighteen years of age, doctor," observed Mrs. Melmoth, "and she has cause to be thankful that she will have better instruction than yours."

This was a proposition that Dr. Melmoth did not choose to dispute; though he perhaps thought that his long and successful experience in the education of the other sex might make him an able coadjutor to his wife in the care of Ellen Langton. He determined to journey in person to the seaport where his young charge resided, leaving the concerns of Harley College to the direction of the two tutors. Mrs. Melmoth, who, indeed, anticipated with pleasure the arrival of a new subject to her authority, threw no difficulties in the way of his intention. To do her justice, her preparations for his journey, and the minute instructions with which she favored him, were such as only a woman's true affection could have suggested. The traveller met with no incidents important to this tale; and, after an absence of about a fortnight, he and Ellen alighted from their steeds (for on horseback had the journey been performed) in safety at his own door.

If pen could give an adequate idea of Ellen Langton's loveliness, it would achieve what pencil (the pencils, at least, of the colonial artists who attempted it) never could; for, though the dark eyes might be painted, the pure and pleasant thoughts that peeped through them could only be seen and felt. But descriptions of beauty are never satisfactory. It must, therefore, be left to the imagination of the reader to conceive of something not more than mortal, nor, indeed, quite the perfection of mortality, but charming men the more, because they felt, that, lovely as she was, she was of like nature to themselves.

From the time that Ellen entered Dr. Melmoth's habitation, the sunny days seemed brighter and the cloudy ones less gloomy, than he had ever before known them. He naturally delighted in children; and Ellen, though her years approached to womanhood, had yet much of the gayety and simple happiness, because the innocence, of a child. She consequently became the very blessing of his life,—the rich recreation that he promised himself for hours of literary toil. On one occasion, indeed, he even made her his companion in the sacred retreat of his study, with the purpose of entering upon a course of instruction in the learned languages. This measure, however, he found inexpedient to repeat; for Ellen, having discovered an old romance among his heavy folios, contrived, by the charm of her sweet voice, to engage his attention therein till all more important concerns were forgotten.

With Mrs. Melmoth, Ellen was not, of course, so great a favorite as with her husband; for women cannot so readily as men, bestow upon the offspring of others those affections that nature intended for their own; and the doctor's extraordinary partiality was anything rather than a pledge of his wife's. But Ellen differed so far from the idea she had previously formed of her, as a daughter of one of the principal merchants, who were then, as now, like nobles in the land, that the stock of dislike which Mrs. Melmoth had provided was found to be totally inapplicable. The young stranger strove so hard, too (and undoubtedly it was a pleasant labor), to win her love, that she was successful to a degree of which the lady herself was not, perhaps, aware. It was soon seen that her education had not been neglected in those points which Mrs. Melmoth deemed most important. The nicer departments of cookery, after sufficient proof of her skill, were committed to her care; and the doctor's table was now covered with delicacies, simple indeed, but as tempting on account of their intrinsic excellence as of the small white hands that made them. By such arts as these,— which in her were no arts, but the dictates of an affectionate disposition,—by making herself useful where it was possible, and agreeable on all occasions, Ellen gained the love of everyone within the sphere of her influence.

But the maiden's conquests were not confined to the members of Dr. Melmoth's family. She had numerous admirers among those whose situation compelled them to stand afar off, and gaze upon her loveliness, as if she were a star, whose brightness they saw, but whose warmth they could not feel. These were the young men of Harley College, whose chief opportunities of beholding Ellen were upon the Sabbaths, when she worshipped with them in the little chapel, which served the purposes of a church to all the families of the vicinity. There was, about this period (and the fact was undoubtedly attributable to Ellen's influence,) a general and very evident decline in the scholarship of the college, especially in regard to the severer studies. The intellectual powers of the young men seemed to be directed chiefly to the construction of Latin and Greek verse, many copies of which, with a characteristic and classic gallantry, were strewn in the path where Ellen Langton was accustomed to walk. They, however, produced no perceptible effect; nor were the aspirations of another ambitious youth, who celebrated her perfections in Hebrew, attended with their merited success.

But there was one young man, to whom circumstances, independent of his personal advantages, afforded a superior opportunity of gaining Ellen's favor. He was nearly related to Dr. Melmoth, on which account he received his education at Harley College, rather than at one of the English universities, to the expenses of which his fortune would have been adequate. This connection entitled him to a frequent and familiar access to the domestic hearth of the dignitary,—an advantage of which, since Ellen Langton became a member of the family, he very constantly availed himself.

Edward Walcott was certainly much superior, in most of the particulars of which a lady takes cognizance, to those of his fellow-students who had come under Ellen's notice. He was tall; and the natural grace of his manners had been improved (an advantage which few of his associates could boast) by early intercourse with polished society. His features, also, were handsome, and promised to be manly and dignified when they should cease to be youthful. His character as a scholar was more than respectable, though many youthful follies, sometimes, perhaps, approaching near to vices, were laid to his charge. But his occasional derelictions from discipline were not such as to create any very serious apprehensions respecting his future welfare; nor were they greater than, perhaps, might be expected from a young man who possessed a considerable command of money, and who was, besides, the fine gentleman of the little community of which he was a member,—a character which generally leads its possessor into follies that he would otherwise have avoided.

With this youth Ellen Langton became familiar, and even intimate; for he was her only companion, of an age suited to her own, and the difference of sex did not occur to her as an objection. He was her constant companion on all necessary and allowable occasions, and drew upon himself, in consequence, the envy of the college.

CHAPTER II

"Why, all delights are vain, but that most vain,
Which, with pain purchased, doth inherit pain:
As painfully to pore upon a book
To seek the light of truth, while truth, the while,
Doth falsely blind the eyesight of his look."

SHAKESPEARE.

ON one of the afternoons which afforded to the students a relaxation from their usual labors, Ellen was attended by her cavalier in a little excursion over the rough bridle-roads that led from her new residence. She was an experienced equestrian,—a necessary accomplishment at that period, when vehicles of every kind were rare. It was now the latter end of spring; but the season had hitherto been backward, with only a few warm and pleasant days. The present afternoon, however, was a delicious mingling of spring and summer, forming in their union an atmosphere so mild and pure, that to breathe was almost a positive happiness. There was a little alternation of cloud across the brow of heaven, but only so much as to render the sunshine more delightful.

The path of the young travellers lay sometimes among tall and thick standing trees, and sometimes over naked and desolate hills, whence man had taken the natural vegetation, and then left the soil to its barrenness. Indeed, there is little inducement to a cultivator to labor among the huge stones which there peep forth from the earth, seeming to form a continued ledge for several miles. A singular contrast to this unfavored tract of country is seen in the narrow but luxuriant, though sometimes swampy, strip of interval, on both sides of the stream, that, as has been noticed, flows down the valley. The light and buoyant spirits of Edward Walcott and Ellen rose higher as they rode on; and their way was enlivened, wherever its roughness did not forbid, by their conversation and pleasant laughter. But at length Ellen drew her bridle, as they emerged from a thick portion of the forest, just at the foot of a steep hill.

"We must have ridden far," she observed,—"farther than I thought. It will be near sunset before we can reach home."

"There are still several hours of daylight," replied Edward Walcott; "and we will not turn back without ascending this hill. The prospect from the summit is beautiful, and will be particularly so now, in this rich sunlight. Come, Ellen,—one light touch of the whip,—your pony is as fresh as when we started."

On reaching the summit of the hill, and looking back in the direction in which they had come, they could see the little stream, peeping forth many times to the daylight, and then shrinking back into the shade. Farther on, it became broad and deep, though rendered incapable of navigation, in this part of its course, by the occasional interruption of rapids.

"There are hidden wonders of rock and precipice and cave, in that dark forest," said Edward, pointing to the space between them and the river. "If it were earlier in the day, I should love to lead you there. Shall we try the adventure now, Ellen?"

"Oh no!" she replied. "Let us delay no longer. I fear I must even now abide a rebuke from Mrs. Melmoth, which I have surely deserved. But who is this, who rides on so slowly before us?"

She pointed to a horseman, whom they had not before observed. He was descending the hill; but, as his steed seemed to have chosen his own pace, he made a very inconsiderable progress.

"Oh, do you not know him? But it is scarcely possible you should," exclaimed her companion. "We must do him the good office, Ellen, of stopping his progress, or he will find himself at the village, a dozen miles farther on, before he resumes his consciousness."

"Has he then lost his senses?" inquired Miss Langton.

"Not so, Ellen,—if much learning has not made him mad," replied Edward Walcott. "He is a deep scholar and a noble fellow; but I fear we shall follow him to his grave erelong. Dr. Melmoth has sent him to ride in pursuit of his health. He will never overtake it, however, at this pace."

As he spoke, they had approached close to the subject of their conversation; and Ellen had a moment's space for observation before he started from the abstraction in which he was plunged. The result of her scrutiny was favorable, yet very painful.

The stranger could scarcely have attained his twentieth year, and was possessed of a face and form such as Nature bestows on none but her favorites. There was a nobleness on his high forehead, which time would have deepened into majesty; and all his features were formed with a strength and boldness, of which the paleness, produced by study and confinement, could not deprive them. The expression of his countenance was not a melancholy one: on the contrary, it was proud and high, perhaps triumphant, like one who was a ruler in a world of his own, and independent of the beings that surrounded him. But a blight, of which his thin pale cheek, and the brightness of his eye, were alike proofs, seemed to have come over him ere his maturity.

The scholar's attention was now aroused by the hoof-tramps at his side; and, starting, he fixed his eyes on Ellen, whose young and lovely countenance was full of the interest he had excited. A deep blush immediately suffused his cheek, proving how well the glow of health would have become it. There was nothing awkward, however, in his manner; and, soon recovering his self-possession, he bowed to her, and would have rode on.

"Your ride is unusually long to-day, Fanshawe," observed Edward Walcott. "When may we look for your return?"

The young man again blushed, but answered, with a smile that had a beautiful effect upon his countenance, "I was not, at the moment, aware in which direction my horse's head was turned. I have to thank you for arresting me in a journey which was likely to prove much longer than I intended."

The party had now turned their horses, and were about to resume their ride in a homeward direction; but Edward perceived that Fanshawe, having lost the excitement of intense thought, now looked weary and dispirited.

"Here is a cottage close at hand," he observed. "We have ridden far, and stand in need of refreshment. Ellen, shall we alight?"

She saw the benevolent motive of his proposal, and did not hesitate to comply with it. But, as they paused at the cottage door, she could not but observe that its exterior promised few of the comforts which they required. Time and neglect seemed to have conspired for its ruin; and, but for a thin curl of smoke from its clay chimney, they could not have believed it to be inhabited. A considerable tract of land in the vicinity of the cottage had evidently been, at some former period, under cultivation, but was now overrun by bushes and dwarf pines, among which many huge gray rocks, ineradicable by human art, endeavored to conceal themselves. About half an acre of ground was occupied by the young blades of Indian-corn, at which a half-starved cow gazed wistfully over the mouldering log-fence. These were the only agricultural tokens. Edward Walcott, nevertheless, drew the latch of the cottage door, after knocking loudly but in vain.

The apartment which was thus opened to their view was quite as wretched as its exterior had given them reason to anticipate. Poverty was there, with all its necessary and unnecessary concomitants. The intruders would have retired had not the hope of affording relief detained them.

The occupants of the small and squalid apartment were two women, both of them elderly, and, from the resemblance of their features, appearing to be sisters. The expression of their countenances, however, was very different. One, evidently the younger, was seated on the farther side of the large hearth, opposite to the door at which the party stood. She had the sallow look of long and wasting illness; and there was an unsteadiness of expression about her eyes, that immediately struck the observer. Yet her face was mild and gentle, therein contrasting widely with that of her companion.

The other woman was bending over a small fire of decayed branches, the flame of which was very disproportionate to the smoke, scarcely producing heat sufficient for the preparation of a scanty portion of food. Her profile only was visible to the strangers, though, from a slight motion of her eye, they perceived that she was aware of their presence. Her features were pinched and spare, and wore a look of sullen discontent, for which the evident wretchedness of her situation afforded a sufficient reason. This female, notwithstanding her years, and the habitual fretfulness (that is more wearing than time), was apparently healthy and robust, with a dry, leathery complexion. A short space elapsed before she thought proper to turn her face towards her visitors; and she then regarded them with a lowering eye, without speaking, or rising from her chair.

"We entered," Edward Walcott began to say, "in the hope"—But he paused, on perceiving that the sick woman had risen from her seat, and with slow and tottering footsteps was drawing near to him. She took his hand in both her own; and, though he shuddered at the touch of age and disease, he did not attempt to withdraw it. She then perused all his features, with an expression, at first of eager and hopeful anxiety, which faded by degrees into disappointment. Then, turning from him, she gazed into Fanshawe's countenance with the like eagerness, but with the same result. Lastly, tottering back to her chair, she hid her face and wept bitterly. The strangers, though they knew not the cause of her grief, were deeply affected; and Ellen approached the mourner with words of comfort, which, more from their tone than their meaning, produced a transient effect.

"Do you bring news of him?" she inquired, raising her head. "Will he return to me? Shall I see him before I die?" Ellen knew not what to answer; and, ere she could attempt it, the other female prevented her.

"Sister Butler is wandering in her mind," she said, "and speaks of one she will never behold again. The sight of strangers disturbs her, and you see we have nothing here to offer you."

The manner of the woman was ungracious; but her words were true. They saw that their presence could do nothing towards the alleviation of the misery they witnessed; and they felt that mere curiosity would not authorize a longer intrusion. So soon, therefore, as they had relieved, according to their power, the poverty that seemed to be the least evil of this cottage, they emerged into the open air.

The breath of heaven felt sweet to them, and removed a part of the weight from their young hearts, which were saddened by the sight of so much wretchedness. Perceiving a pure and bright little fountain at a short distance from the cottage, they approached it, and, using the bark of a birch-tree as a cup, partook of its cool waters. They then pursued their homeward ride with such diligence, that, just as the sun was setting, they came in sight of the humble wooden edifice which was dignified with the name of Harley College. A golden ray rested upon the spire of the little chapel, the bell of which sent its tinkling murmur down the valley to summon the wanderers to evening prayers.

Fanshawe returned to his chamber that night, and lighted his lamp as he had been wont to do. The books were around him which had hitherto been to him like those fabled volumes of Magic, from which the reader could not turn away his eye till death were the consequence of his studies. But there were unaccustomed thoughts in his bosom now; and to these, leaning his head on one of the unopened volumes, he resigned himself.

He called up in review the years, that, even at his early age, he had spent in solitary study, in conversation with the dead, while he had scorned to mingle with the living world, or to be actuated by any of its motives. He asked himself to what purpose was all this destructive labor, and where was the happiness of superior knowledge. He had climbed but a few steps of a ladder that reached to infinity: he had thrown away his life in discovering, that, after a thousand such lives, he should still know comparatively nothing. He even looked forward with dread—though once the thought had been dear to him—to the eternity of improvement that lay before him. It seemed now a weary way, without a resting-place and without a termination; and at that moment he would have preferred the dreamless sleep of the brutes that perish to man's proudest attribute,—of immortality.

Fanshawe had hitherto deemed himself unconnected with the world, Unconcerned in its feelings, and uninfluenced by it in any of its pursuits. In this respect he probably deceived himself. If his inmost heart could have been laid open, there would have been discovered that dream of undying fame, which, dream as it is, is more powerful than a thousand realities. But, at any rate, he had seemed, to others and to himself, a solitary being, upon whom the hopes and fears of ordinary men were ineffectual.

But now he felt the first thrilling of one of the many ties, that, so long as we breathe the common air, (and who shall say how much longer?) unite us to our kind. The sound of a soft, sweet voice, the glance of a gentle eye, had wrought a change upon him; and in his ardent mind a few hours had done the work of many. Almost in spite of himself, the new sensation was inexpressibly delightful. The recollection of his ruined health, of his habits (so much at variance with those of the world),—all the difficulties that reason suggested, were inadequate to check the exulting tide of hope and joy.

CHAPTER III

"And let the aspiring youth beware of love,—
Of the smooth glance beware; for 'tis too late
When on his heart the torrent softness pours;
Then wisdom prostrate lies, and fading fame
Dissolves in air away."

THOMSON

A FEW months passed over the heads of Ellen Langton and her admirers, unproductive of events, that, separately, were of sufficient importance to be related. The summer was now drawing to a close; and Dr. Melmoth had received information that his friend's arrangements were nearly completed, and that by the next home-bound ship he hoped to return to his native country. The arrival of that ship was daily expected.

During the time that had elapsed since his first meeting with Ellen, there had been a change, yet not a very remarkable one, in Fanshawe's habits. He was still the same solitary being, so far as regarded his own sex; and he still confined himself as sedulously to his chamber, except for one hour—the sunset hour—of every day. At that period, unless prevented by the inclemency of the weather, he was accustomed to tread a path that wound along the banks of the stream. He had discovered that this was the most frequent scene of Ellen's walks; and this it was that drew him thither.

Their intercourse was at first extremely slight,—a bow on the one side, a smile on the other, and a passing word from both; and then the student hurried back to his solitude. But, in course of time, opportunities occurred for more extended conversation; so that, at the period with which this chapter is concerned, Fanshawe was, almost as constantly as Edward Walcott himself, the companion of Ellen's walks.

His passion had strengthened more than proportionably to the time that had elapsed since it was conceived; but the first glow and excitement which attended it had now vanished. He had reasoned calmly with himself, and rendered evident to his own mind the almost utter hopelessness of success. He had also made his resolution strong, that he would not even endeavor to win Ellen's love, the result of which, for a thousand reasons, could not be happiness. Firm in this determination, and confident of his power to adhere to it; feeling, also, that time and absence could not cure his own passion, and having no desire for such a cure,—he saw no reason for breaking off the intercourse that was established between Ellen and himself. It was remarkable, that, notwithstanding the desperate nature of his love, that, or something connected with it, seemed to have a beneficial effect upon his health. There was now a slight tinge of color in his cheek, and a less consuming brightness in his eye. Could it be that hope, unknown to himself, was yet alive in his breast; that a sense of the possibility of earthly happiness was redeeming him from the grave?

Had the character of Ellen Langton's mind been different, there might, perhaps, have been danger to her from an intercourse of this nature with such a being as Fanshawe; for he was distinguished by many of those asperities around which a woman's affection will often cling. But she was formed to walk in the calm and quiet paths of life, and to pluck the flowers of happiness from the wayside where they grow. Singularity of character, therefore, was not calculated to win her love. She undoubtedly felt an interest in the solitary student, and perceiving, with no great exercise of vanity, that her society drew him from the destructive intensity of his studies, she perhaps felt it a duty to exert her influence. But it did not occur to her that her influence had been sufficiently strong to change the whole current of his thoughts and feelings.

Ellen and her two lovers (for both, though perhaps not equally, deserved that epithet) had met, as usual, at the close of a sweet summer day, and were standing by the side of the stream, just where it swept into a deep pool. The current, undermining the bank, had formed a recess, which, according to Edward Walcott, afforded at that moment a hiding-place to a trout of noble size.

"Now would I give the world," he exclaimed with great interest, "for a hook and line, a fish-spear, or any piscatorial instrument of death! Look, Ellen, you can see the waving of his tail from beneath the bank!"

"If you had the means of taking him, I should save him from your cruelty, thus," said Ellen, dropping a pebble into the water, just over the fish. "There! he has darted down the stream. How many pleasant caves and recesses there must be under these banks, where he may be happy! May there not be happiness in the life of a fish?" she added, turning with a smile to Fanshawe.

"There may," he replied, "so long as he lives quietly in the caves and recesses of which you speak, Yes, there may be happiness, though such as few would envy; but, then, the hook and line"—

"Which, there is reason to apprehend, will shortly destroy the happiness of our friend the trout," interrupted Edward, pointing down the stream. "There is an angler on his way toward us, who will intercept him."

"He seems to care little for the sport, to judge by the pace at which he walks," said Ellen.

"But he sees, now, that we are observing him, and is willing to prove that he knows something of the art," replied Edward Walcott. "I should think him well acquainted with the stream; for, hastily as he walks, he has tried every pool and ripple where a fish usually hides. But that point will be decided when he reaches yonder old bare oak-tree."

"And how is the old tree to decide the question?" inquired Fanshawe. "It is a species of evidence of which I have never before heard."

"The stream has worn a hollow under its roots," answered Edward,—"a most delicate retreat for a trout. Now, a stranger would not discover the spot; or, if he did, the probable result of a cast would be the loss of hook and line,—an accident that has occurred to me more than once. If, therefore, this angler takes a fish from thence, it follows that he knows the stream."

They observed the fisher, accordingly, as he kept his way up the bank. He did not pause when he reached the old leafless oak, that formed with its roots an obstruction very common in American streams; but, throwing his line with involuntary skill as he passed, he not only escaped the various entanglements, but drew forth a fine large fish.

"There, Ellen, he has captivated your *protégé*, the trout, or, at least, one very like him in size," observed Edward. "It is singular," he added, gazing earnestly at the man.

"Why is it singular?" inquired Ellen Langton. "This person, perhaps, resides in the neighborhood, and may have fished often in the stream."

"Do but look at him, Ellen, and judge whether his life can have been spent in this lonely valley," he replied. "The glow of many a hotter sun than ours has darkened his brow; and his step and air have something foreign in them, like what we see in sailors who have lived more in other countries than in their own. Is it not so, Ellen? for your education in a seaport must have given you skill in these matters. But come, let us approach nearer."

They walked towards the angler, accordingly, who still remained under the oak, apparently engaged in arranging his fishing-tackle. As the party drew nigh, he raised his head, and threw one quick, scrutinizing glance towards them, disclosing, on his part, a set of bold and rather coarse features, weather-beaten, but indicating the age of the owner to be not above thirty. In person he surpassed the middle size, was well set, and evidently strong and active.

"Do you meet with much success, sir?" inquired Edward Walcott, when within a convenient distance for conversation.

"I have taken but one fish," replied the angler, in an accent which his hearers could scarcely determine to be foreign, or the contrary. "I am a stranger to the stream, and have doubtless passed over many a likely place for sport."

"You have an angler's eye, sir," rejoined Edward.

"I observed that you made your casts as if you had often trod these banks, and I could scarcely have guided you better myself."

"Yes, I have learned the art, and I love to practise it," replied the man. "But will not the young lady try her skill?" he

NATHANIEL HAWTHORNE

continued, casting a bold eye on Ellen. "The fish will love to be drawn out by such white hands as those."

Ellen shrank back, though almost imperceptibly, from the free bearing of the man. It seemed meant for courtesy; but its effect was excessively disagreeable. Edward Walcott, who perceived and coincided in Ellen's feelings, replied to the stranger's proposal.

"The young lady will not put the gallantry of the fish to the proof, sir," he said, "and she will therefore have no occasion for your own."

"I shall take leave to hear my answer from the young lady's own mouth," answered the stranger, haughtily. "If you will step this way, Miss Langton" (here he interrupted himself),— "if you will cast the line by yonder sunken log, I think you will meet with success."

Thus saying, the angler offered his rod and line to Ellen. She at first drew back, then hesitated, but finally held out her hand to receive them. In thus complying with the stranger's request, she was actuated by a desire to keep the peace, which, as her notice of Edward Walcott's crimsoned cheek and flashing eye assured her, was considerably endangered. The angler led the way to the spot which he had pointed out, which, though not at such a distance from Ellen's companions but that words in a common tone could be distinguished, was out of the range of a lowered voice.

Edward Walcott and the student remained by the oak: the former biting his lip with vexation; the latter, whose abstraction always vanished where Ellen was concerned, regarding her and the stranger with fixed and silent attention. The young men could at first hear the words that the angler addressed to Ellen. They related to the mode of managing the rod; and she made one or two casts under his direction. At length, however, as if to offer his assistance, the man advanced close to her side, and seemed to speak, but in so low a tone, that the sense of what he uttered was lost before it reached the oak. But its effect upon Ellen was immediate and very obvious. Her eyes flashed; and an indignant blush rose high on her cheek, giving to her beauty a haughty brightness, of which the gentleness of her disposition in general deprived it. The next moment, however, she seemed to recollect herself, and, restoring the angling-rod to its owner, she turned away calmly, and approached her companions.

"The evening breeze grows chill; and mine is a dress for a summer day," she observed. "Let us walk homeward."

"Miss Langton, is it the evening breeze alone that sends you homeward?" inquired Edward.

At this moment the angler, who had resumed, and seemed to be intent upon his occupation, drew a fish from the pool, which he had pointed out to Ellen.

"I told the young lady," he exclaimed, "that, if she would listen to me a moment longer, she would be repaid for her trouble; and here is the proof of my words."

"Come, let us hasten towards home," cried Ellen, eagerly; and she took Edward Walcott's arm, with a freedom that, at another time, would have enchanted him. He at first seemed inclined to resist her wishes, but complied, after exchanging, unperceived by Ellen, a glance with the stranger, the meaning of which the latter appeared perfectly to understand. Fanshawe also attended her. Their walk towards Dr. Melmoth's dwelling was almost a silent one; and the few words that passed between them did not relate to the adventure which occupied the thoughts of each. On arriving at the house, Ellen's attendants took leave of her, and retired.

Edward Walcott, eluding Fanshawe's observation with little difficulty, hastened back to the old oak-tree. From the intelligence with which the stranger had received his meaning glance, the young man had supposed that he would here await his return. But the banks of the stream, upward and downward, so far as his eye could reach, were solitary. He could see only his own image in the water, where it swept into a silent depth; and could hear only its ripple, where stones and sunken trees impeded its course. The object of his search might, indeed, have found concealment among the tufts of alders, or in the forest that was near at hand; but thither it was in vain to pursue him. The angler had apparently set little store by the fruits of his assumed occupation; for the last fish that he had taken lay, yet alive, on the bank, gasping for the element to which Edward was sufficiently compassionate to restore him.

After watching him as he glided down the stream, making feeble efforts to resist its current, the youth turned away, and sauntered slowly towards the college.

Ellen Langton, on her return from her walk, found Dr. Melmoth's little parlor unoccupied; that gentleman being deeply engaged in his study, and his lady busied in her domestic affairs. The evening, notwithstanding Ellen's remark concerning the chillness of the breeze, was almost sultry; and the windows of the apartment were thrown open. At one of these, which looked into the garden, she seated herself, listening, almost unconsciously, to the monotonous music of a thousand insects, varied occasionally by the voice of a whippoorwill, who, as the day departed, was just commencing his song. A dusky tint, as yet almost imperceptible, was beginning to settle on the surrounding objects, except where they were opposed to the purple and golden clouds, which the vanished sun had made the brief inheritors of a portion of his brightness. In these gorgeous vapors, Ellen's fancy, in the interval of other thoughts, pictured a fairy-land, and longed for wings to visit it.

But as the clouds lost their brilliancy, and assumed first a dull purple, and then a sullen gray tint, Ellen's thoughts recurred to the adventure of the angler, which her imagination was inclined to invest with an undue singularity. It was, however, sufficiently unaccountable that an entire stranger should venture to demand of her a private audience; and she assigned, in turn, a thousand motives for such a request, none of which were in any degree satisfactory. Her most prevailing thought, though she could not justify it to her reason, inclined her to believe that the angler was a messenger from her father. But wherefore he should deem it necessary to communicate any intelligence that he might possess only by means of a private interview, and without the knowledge of her friends, was a mystery she could not solve. In this view of the matter, however, she half regretted that her instinctive delicacy had impelled her so suddenly to break off their conference, admitting, in the secrecy of her own mind, that, if an opportunity were again to occur, it might not again be shunned. As if that unuttered thought had power to conjure up its object, she now became aware of a form standing in the garden, at a short distance from the window where she sat. The dusk had deepened, during Ellen's abstraction, to such a degree, that the man's features were not perfectly distinguishable; but the maiden was not long in doubt of his identity, for he approached, and spoke in the same low tone in which he had addressed her when they stood by the stream.

"Do you still refuse my request, when its object is but your own good, and that of one who should be most dear to you?" he asked.

Ellen's first impulse had been to cry out for assistance; her second was to fly: but, rejecting both these measures, she determined to remain, endeavoring to persuade herself that she was safe. The quivering of her voice, however, when she attempted to reply, betrayed her apprehensions.

"I cannot listen to such a request from a stranger," she said. "If you bring news from—from my father, why is it not told to Dr. Melmoth?"

"Because what I have to say is for your ear alone," was the reply; "and if you would avoid misfortune now, and sorrow hereafter, you will not refuse to hear me."

"And does it concern my father?" asked Ellen, eagerly.

"It does—most deeply," answered the stranger.

She meditated a moment, and then replied, "I will not refuse, I will hear—but speak quickly."

"We are in danger of interruption in this place, and that would be fatal to my errand," said the stranger. "I will await you in the garden."

With these words, and giving her no opportunity for reply, he drew back; and his form faded from her eyes. This precipitate retreat from argument was the most probable method that he could have adopted of gaining his end. He had awakened the strongest interest in Ellen's mind; and he calculated justly in supposing that she would consent to an interview upon his own terms.

Dr. Melmoth had followed his own fancies in the mode of laying out his garden; and, in consequence, the plan that had undoubtedly existed in his mind was utterly incomprehensible to every one but himself. It was an intermixture of kitchen and flower garden, a labyrinth of winding paths, bordered by hedges, and impeded by shrubbery. Many of the original trees of the forest were still flourishing among the exotics which the doctor had transplanted thither. It was not without a sensation of fear, stronger than she had ever before experienced, that Ellen Langton found herself in this artificial wilderness, and in the presence of the mysterious stranger. The dusky light deepened the lines of his dark, strong features; and Ellen fancied that his countenance wore a wilder and a fiercer look than when she had met him by the stream. He perceived her agitation, and addressed her in the softest tones of which his voice was capable.

"Compose yourself," he said; "you have nothing to fear from me. But we are in open view from the house, where we now stand; and discovery would not be without danger to both of us."

"No eye can see us here," said Ellen, trembling at the truth of her own observation, when they stood beneath a gnarled, low-branched pine, which Dr. Melmoth's ideas of beauty had caused him to retain in his garden. "Speak quickly; for I dare follow you no farther."

The spot was indeed sufficiently solitary; and the stranger delayed no longer to explain his errand.

"Your father," he began,—"do you not love him? Would you do aught for his welfare?"

"Everything that a father could ask I would do," exclaimed Ellen, eagerly. "Where is my father? and when shall I meet him?"

"It must depend upon yourself, whether you shall meet him in a few days or never."

"Never!" repeated Ellen. "Is he ill? Is he in danger?"

"He is in danger," replied the man, "but not from illness. Your father is a ruined man. Of all his friends, but one remains to him. That friend has travelled far to prove if his daughter has a daughter's affection."

"And what is to be the proof?" asked Ellen, with more calmness than the stranger had anticipated; for she possessed a large fund of plain sense, which revolted against the mystery of these proceedings. Such a course, too, seemed discordant with her father's character, whose strong mind and almost cold heart were little likely to demand, or even to pardon, the romance of affection.

"This letter will explain," was the reply to Ellen's question. "You will see that it is in your father's hand; and that may gain your confidence, though I am doubted."

She received the letter; and many of her suspicions of the stranger's truth were vanquished by the apparent openness of his manner. He was preparing to speak further, but paused, for a footstep was now heard, approaching from the lower part of the garden. From their situation,—at some distance from the path, and in the shade of the tree,—they had a fair chance of eluding discovery from any unsuspecting passenger; and, when Ellen saw that the intruder was Fanshawe, she hoped that his usual abstraction would assist their concealment.

But, as the student advanced along the path, his air was not that of one whose deep inward thoughts withdrew his attention from all outward objects. He rather resembled the hunter, on the watch for his game; and, while he was yet at a distance from Ellen, a wandering gust of wind waved her white garment, and betrayed her.

"It is as I feared," said Fanshawe to himself. He then drew nigh, and addressed Ellen with a calm authority that became him well, notwithstanding that his years scarcely exceeded her own. "Miss Langton," he inquired, "what do you here at such an hour, and with such a companion?"

Ellen was sufficiently displeased at what she deemed the unauthorized intrusion of Fanshawe in her affairs; but his imposing manner and her own confusion prevented her from replying.

"Permit me to lead you to the house," he continued, in the words of a request, but in the tone of a command. "The dew hangs dank and heavy on these branches; and a longer stay would be more dangerous than you are aware."

Ellen would fain have resisted; but though the tears hung as heavy on her eyelashes, between shame and anger, as the dew upon the leaves, she felt compelled to accept the arm that he offered her. But the stranger, who, since Fanshawe's approach, had remained a little apart, now advanced.

"You speak as one in authority, young man," he said. "Have you the means of compelling obedience? Does your power extend to men? Or do you rule only over simple girls? Miss Langton is under my protection, and, till you can bend me to your will, she shall remain so."

Fanshawe turned calmly, and fixed his eyes on the stranger. "Retire, sir," was all he said.

Ellen almost shuddered, as if there were a mysterious and unearthly power in Fanshawe's voice; for she saw that the stranger endeavored in vain, borne down by the influence of a superior mind, to maintain the boldness of look and bearing that seemed natural to him. He at first made a step forward, then muttered a few half-audible words; but, quailing at length beneath the young man's bright and steady eye, he turned and slowly withdrew.

Fanshawe remained silent a moment after his opponent had departed, and, when he next spoke, it was in a tone of depression. Ellen observed, also, that his countenance had lost its look of pride and authority; and he seemed faint and exhausted. The occasion that called forth his energies had passed; and they had left him.

"Forgive me, Miss Langton," he said almost humbly, "if my eagerness to serve you has led me too far. There is evil in this stranger, more than your pure mind can conceive. I know not what has been his errand; but let me entreat you to put confidence in those to whose care your father has intrusted you. Or if I—or—or Edward Walcott—But I have no right to advise you; and your own calm thoughts will guide you best."

He said no more; and, as Ellen did not reply, they reached the house, and parted in silence.

CHAPTER IV

"The seeds by nature planted
Take a deep root in the soil, and though for a time
The trenchant share and tearing harrow may
Sweep all appearance of them from the surface,
Yet with the first warm rains of spring they'll shoot,
And with their rankness smother the good grain.
Heaven grant, it mayn't be so with him."

RICHES.

THE scene of this tale must now be changed to the little inn, which at that period, as at the present, was situated in the vicinity of Harley College. The site of the modern establishment is the same with that of the ancient; but everything of the latter that had been built by hands has gone to decay and been removed, and only the earth beneath and around it remains the same. The modern building, a house of two stories, after a lapse of twenty years, is yet unfinished. On this account, it has retained the appellation of the "New Inn," though, like many who have frequented it, it has grown old ere its maturity. Its dingy whiteness, and its apparent superfluity of windows (many of them being closed with rough boards), give it somewhat of a dreary look, especially in a wet day.

The ancient inn was a house, of which the eaves approached within about seven feet of the ground; while the roof, sloping gradually upward, formed an angle at several times that height. It was a comfortable and pleasant abode to the weary traveller, both in summer and winter; for the frost never ventured within the sphere of its huge hearths; and it was protected from the heat of the sultry season by three large elms that swept the roof with their long branches, and seemed to create a breeze where there was not one. The device upon the sign, suspended from one of these trees, was a hand holding a long-necked bottle, and was much more appropriate than the present unmeaning representation of a black eagle. But it is necessary to speak rather more at length of the landlord than of the house over which he presided.

Hugh Crombie was one for whom most of the wise men, who considered the course of his early years, had predicted the gallows as an end before he should arrive at middle age. That these prophets of ill had been deceived was evident from the fact that the doomed man had now passed the fortieth year, and was in more prosperous circumstances than most of those who had wagged their tongues against him. Yet the failure of their forebodings was more remarkable than their fulfilment would have been.

He had been distinguished, almost from his earliest infancy, by those precocious accomplishments, which, because they consist in an imitation of the vices and follies of maturity, render a boy the favorite plaything of men. He seemed to have received from nature the convivial talents, which, whether natural or acquired, are a most dangerous possession; and, before his twelfth year, he was the welcome associate of all the idle and dissipated of his neighborhood, and especially of those who haunted the tavern of which he had now become the landlord. Under this course of education, Hugh Crombie grew to youth and manhood; and the lovers of good words could only say in his favor, that he was a greater enemy to himself than to any one else, and that, if he should reform, few would have a better chance of prosperity than he.

The former clause of this modicum of praise (if praise it may be termed) was indisputable; but it may be doubted, whether, under any circumstances where his success depended on his own exertions, Hugh would have made his way well through the world. He was one of those unfortunate persons, who, instead of being perfect in any single art or occupation, are superficial in many, and who are supposed to possess a larger share of talent than other men, because it consists of numerous scraps, instead of a single mass. He was partially acquainted with most of the manual arts that gave bread to others; but not one of them, nor all of them, would give bread to him. By some fatality, the only two of his multifarious accomplishments in which his excellence was generally conceded were both calculated to keep him poor rather than to make him rich. He was a musician and a poet. There are yet remaining in that portion of the country many ballads and songs,—set to their own peculiar tunes,—the authorship of which is attributed to him. In general, his productions were upon subjects of local and temporary interest, and would consequently require a bulk of explanatory notes to render them interesting or intelligible to the world at large. A considerable proportion of the remainder are Anacreontics; though, in their construction, Hugh Crombie imitated neither the Teian nor any other bard. These latter have generally a coarseness and sensuality intolerable to minds even of no very fastidious delicacy. But there are two or three simple little songs, into which a feeling and a natural pathos have found their way, that still retain their influence over the heart. These, after two or three centuries, may perhaps be precious to the collectors of our early poetry. At any rate, Hugh Crombie's effusions, tavern-haunter and vagrant though he was, have gained a continuance of fame (confined, indeed, to a narrow section of the country), which many who called themselves poets then, and would have scorned such a brother, have failed to equal.

During the long winter evenings, when the farmers were idle round their hearths, Hugh was a courted guest; for none could while away the hours more skilfully than he. The winter, therefore, was his season of prosperity; in which respect he differed from the butterflies and useless insects, to which he otherwise bore a resemblance. During the cold months, a very desirable alteration for the better appeared in his outward man. His cheeks were plump and sanguine; his eyes bright and cheerful; and the tip of his nose glowed with a Bardolphian fire,—a flame, indeed, which Hugh was so far a vestal as to supply with its necessary fuel at all seasons of the year. But, as the spring advanced, he assumed a lean and sallow look, wilting and fading in the sunshine that brought life and joy to every animal and vegetable except himself. His winter patrons eyed him with an austere regard; and some even practised upon him the modern and fashionable courtesy of the "cut direct."

Yet, after all, there was good, or something that Nature intended to be so, in the poor outcast,—some lovely flowers, the sweeter even for the weeds that choked them. An instance of this was his affection for an aged father, whose whole support was the broken reed,—his son. Notwithstanding his own necessities, Hugh contrived to provide food and raiment for the old man: how, it would be difficult to say, and perhaps as well not to inquire. He also exhibited traits of sensitiveness to neglect and insult, and of gratitude for favors; both of which feelings a course of life like his is usually quick to eradicate.

At length the restraint—for such his father had ever been—upon Hugh Crombie's conduct was removed by death; and then the wise men and the old began to shake their heads; and they who took pleasure in the follies, vices, and misfortunes of their fellow-creatures, looked for a speedy gratification. They were disappointed, however; for Hugh had apparently determined, that, whatever might be his catastrophe, he would meet it among strangers, rather than at home. Shortly after his father's death, he disappeared altogether from the vicinity; and his name became, in the course of years, an unusual sound, where once the lack of other topics of interest had given it a considerable degree of notoriety. Sometimes, however, when the winter blast was loud round the lonely farm-house, its inmates remembered him who had so often chased away the gloom of such an hour, and, though with little expectation of its fulfilment, expressed a wish to behold him again.

Yet that wish, formed, perhaps, because it appeared so desperate, was finally destined to be gratified. One summer evening, about two years previous to the period of this tale, a man of sober and staid deportment, mounted upon a white horse, arrived at the Hand and Bottle, to which some civil or military meeting had chanced, that day, to draw most of the inhabitants of the vicinity. The stranger was well though plainly dressed, and anywhere but in a retired country town would have attracted no particular attention; but here, where a traveller was not of every-day occurrence, he was soon surrounded by a little crowd, who, when his eye was averted, seized the opportunity diligently to peruse his person. He was rather a thickset man, but with no superfluous flesh; his hair was of iron-gray; he had a few wrinkles; his face was so deeply sunburnt, that, excepting a half-smothered glow on the tip of his nose, a dusky yellow was the only apparent hue. As the people gazed, it was observed that the elderly men, and the men of substance, gat themselves silently to their steeds, and hied homeward with an unusual degree of haste; till at length the inn was deserted, except by a few wretched objects to whom it was a constant resort. These, instead of retreating, drew closer to the traveller, peeping anxiously into his face, and asking, ever and anon, a question, in order to discover the tone of his voice. At length, with one consent, and as if the recognition had at once burst upon them, they hailed their old boon-companion, Hugh Crombie, and, leading him into the inn, did him the honor to partake of a cup of welcome at his expense.

But, though Hugh readily acknowledged the not very reputable acquaintances who alone acknowledged him, they speedily discovered that he was an altered man. He partook with great moderation of the liquor for which he was to pay; he declined all their flattering entreaties for one of his old songs; and finally, being urged to engage in a game at all-fours, he calmly observed, almost in the words of an old clergyman on a like occasion, that his principles forbade a profane appeal to the decision by lot.

On the next Sabbath Hugh Crombie made his appearance at public worship in the chapel of Harley College; and here his outward demeanor was unexceptionably serious and devout,—a praise which, on that particular occasion, could be bestowed on few besides. From these favorable symptoms, the old established prejudices against him began to waver; and as he seemed not to need, and to have no intention to ask, the assistance of any one, he was soon generally acknowledged by the rich as well as by the poor. His account of his past life, and of his intentions for the future, was brief, but not unsatisfactory. He said that, since his departure, he had been a seafaring man, and that, having acquired sufficient property to render him easy in the decline of his days, he had returned to live and die in the town of his nativity.

There was one person, and the one whom Hugh was most interested to please, who seemed perfectly satisfied of the verity of his reformation. This was the landlady of the inn, whom, at his departure, he had left a gay, and, even at thirty-five, a rather pretty wife, and whom, on his return, he found a widow of fifty, fat, yellow, wrinkled, and a zealous member of the church. She, like others, had, at first, cast a cold eye on the wanderer; but it shortly became evident to close observers, that a change was at work in the pious matron's sentiments respecting her old acquaintance. She was now careful to give him his morning dram from her own peculiar bottle, to fill his pipe from her private box of Virginia, and to mix for him the sleeping-cup in which her late husband had delighted. Of all these courtesies Hugh Crombie did partake with a wise and cautious moderation, that, while it proved them to be welcome, expressed his fear of trespassing on her kindness. For the sake of brevity, it shall suffice to say, that, about six weeks after Hugh's return, a writing appeared on one of the elm-trees in front of the tavern (where, as the place of greatest resort, such notices were usually displayed) setting forth that marriage was intended between Hugh Crombie and the Widow Sarah Hutchins. And the ceremony, which made Hugh a landholder, a householder, and a substantial man, in due time took place.

As a landlord, his general conduct was very praiseworthy. He was moderate in his charges, and attentive to his guests; he allowed no gross and evident disorders in his house, and practised none himself; he was kind and charitable to such as needed food and lodging, and had not wherewithal to pay,—for with these his experience had doubtless given him a fellow-feeling. He was also sufficiently attentive to his wife; though it must be acknowledged that the religious zeal which had had a considerable influence in gaining her affections grew, by no moderate degrees, less fervent. It was whispered, too, that the new landlord could, when time, place, and company were to his mind, upraise a song as merrily, and drink a glass as jollily, as in the days of yore. These were the weightiest charges that could now be brought against him; and wise men thought, that, whatever might have been the evil of his past life, he had returned with a desire (which years of vice, if they do not sometimes produce, do not always destroy) of being honest, if opportunity should offer; and Hugh had certainly a fair one.

On the afternoon previous to the events related in the last chapter, the personage whose introduction to the reader has occupied so large a space was seated under one of the elms in front of his dwelling. The bench which now sustained him, and on which were carved the names of many former occupants, was Hugh Crombie's favorite lounging-place, unless when his attentions were required by his guests. No demand had that day been made upon the hospitality of the Hand and Bottle; and the landlord was just then murmuring at the unfrequency of employment. The slenderness of his profits, indeed, were no part of his concern; for the Widow Hutchins's chief income was drawn from her farm, nor was Hugh ever miserly inclined. But his education and habits had made him delight in the atmo-sphere of the inn, and in the society of those who frequented it; and of this species of enjoyment his present situation certainly did not afford an overplus.

Yet had Hugh Crombie an enviable appearance of in-dolence and ease, as he sat under the old tree, polluting the sweet air with his pipe, and taking occasional draughts from a brown jug that stood near at hand. The basis of the potation contained in this vessel was harsh old cider, from the widow's own orchard; but its coldness and acidity were rendered in-nocuous by a due proportion of yet older brandy. The result of this mixture was extremely felicitous, pleasant to the taste, and producing a tingling sensation on the coats of the stomach, uncommonly delectable to so old a toper as Hugh.

The landlord cast his eye, ever and anon, along the road that led down the valley in the direction of the village: and at last, when the sun was wearing west-ward, he discovered the approach of a horseman. He immediately replenished his pipe, took a long draught from the brown jug, summoned the ragged youth who officiated in most of the subordinate depart-ments of the inn, and who was now to act as hostler, and then prepared himself for confabulation with his guest.

"He comes from the sea-coast," said Hugh to himself, as the traveller emerged into open view on the level road. "He is two days in advance of the post, with its news of a fortnight old. Pray Heaven he prove communicative!" Then, as the stranger drew nigher, "One would judge that his dark face had seen as hot a sun as mine. He has felt the burning breeze of the Indies, East and West, I warrant him. Ah, I see we shall send away the evening merrily! Not a penny shall come out of his purse,— that is, if his tongue runs glibly. Just the man I was praying for—Now may the Devil take me if he is!" interrupted Hugh, in accents of alarm, and starting from his seat. He composed his countenance, however, with the power that long habit and necessity had given him over his emotions, and again settled himself quietly on the bench.

The traveller, coming on at a moderate pace, alighted, and gave his horse to the ragged hostler. He then advanced towards the door near which Hugh was seated, whose agitation was manifested by no perceptible sign, except by the shorter and more frequent puffs with which he plied his pipe. Their eyes did not meet till just as the stranger was about to enter, when he started apparently with a surprise and alarm similar to those of Hugh Crombie. He recovered himself, however, sufficiently to return the nod of recognition with which he was favored, and immediately entered the house, the landlord following.

"This way, if you please, sir," said Hugh. "You will find this apartment cool and retired."

He ushered his guest into a small room the windows of which were darkened by the creeping plants that clustered round them. Entering, and closing the door, the two gazed at each other a little space without speaking. The traveller first broke silence.

"Then this is your living self, Hugh Crombie?" he said. The landlord extended his hand as a practical reply to the question. The stranger took it, though with no especial appearance of cordiality.

"Ay, this seems to be flesh and blood," he said, in the tone of one who would willingly have found it otherwise. "And how happens this, friend Hugh? I little thought to meet you again in this life. When I last heard from you, your prayers were said, and you were bound for a better world."

"There would have been small danger of your meeting me there," observed the landlord, dryly.

"It is an unquestionable truth, Hugh," replied the traveller. "For which reason I regret that your voyage was delayed."

"Nay, that is a hard word to bestow on your old comrade," said Hugh Crombie. "The world is wide enough for both of us; and why should you wish me out of it?"

"Wide as it is," rejoined the stranger, "we have stumbled against each other,—to the pleasure of neither of us, if I may judge from your countenance. Methinks I am not a welcome guest at Hugh Crombie's inn."

"Your welcome must depend on the cause of your coming, and the length of your stay," replied the landlord.

"And what if I come to settle down among these quiet hills where I was born?" inquired the other. "What if I, too, am weary of the life we have led,—or afraid, perhaps, that it will come to too speedy an end? Shall I have your good word, Hugh, to set me up in an honest way of life? Or will you make me a partner in your trade, since you know my qualifications? A pretty pair of publicans should we be; and the quart pot would have little rest between us."

"It may be as well to replenish it now," observed Hugh, stepping to the door of the room, and giving orders accordingly. "A meeting between old friends should never be dry. But for the partnership, it is a matter in which you must excuse me. Heaven knows I find it hard enough to be honest, with no tempter but the Devil and my own thoughts; and, if I have you also to contend with, there is little hope of me."

"Nay, that is true. Your good resolutions were always like cobwebs, and your evil habits like five-inch cables," replied the traveller. "I am to understand, then, that you refuse my offer?"

"Not only that; but, if you have chosen this valley as your place of rest, Dame Crombie and I must look through the world for another. But hush! here comes the wine."

The hostler, in the performance of another part of his duty, now appeared, bearing a measure of the liquor that Hugh had ordered. The wine of that period, owing to the comparative lowness of the duties, was of more moderate price than in the mother-country, and of purer and better quality than at the present day.

"The stuff is well chosen, Hugh," observed the guest, after a draught large enough to authorize an opinion. "You have most of the requisites for your present station; and I should be sorry to draw you from it. I trust there will be no need."

"Yet you have a purpose in your journey hither," observed his comrade.

"Yes; and you would fain be informed of it," replied the traveller. He arose, and walked once or twice across the room; then, seeming to have taken his resolution, he paused, and fixed his eye steadfastly on Hugh Crombie. "I could wish, my old acquaintance," he said, "that your lot had been cast anywhere rather than here. Yet, if you choose it, you may do me a good office, and one that shall meet with a good reward. Can I trust you?"

"My secrecy, you can," answered the host, "but nothing further. I know the nature of your plans, and whither they would lead me, too well to engage in them. To say the truth, since it concerns not me, I have little desire to hear your secret."

"And I as little to tell it, I do assure you," rejoined the guest. "I have always loved to manage my affairs myself, and to keep them to myself. It is a good rule; but it must sometimes be broken. And now, Hugh, how is it that you have become possessed of this comfortable dwelling and of these pleasant fields?"

"By my marriage with the Widow Sarah Hutchins," replied Hugh Crombie, staring at a question which seemed to have little reference to the present topic of conversation.

"It is a most excellent method of becoming a man of substance," continued the traveller; "attended with little trouble, and honest withal."

"Why, as to the trouble," said the landlord, "it follows such a bargain, instead of going before it. And for honesty,—I do not recollect that I have gained a penny more honestly these twenty years."

"I can swear to that," observed his comrade. "Well, mine host, I entirely approve of your doings, and, moreover, have resolved to prosper after the same fashion myself."

"If that be the commodity you seek," replied Hugh Crombie, "you will find none here to your mind. We have widows in plenty, it is true; but most of them have children, and few have houses and lands. But now to be serious,—and there has been something serious in your eye all this while,—what is your purpose in coming hither? You are not safe here. Your name has had a wider spread than mine, and, if discovered, it will go hard with you."

"But who would know me now?" asked the guest.

"Few, few indeed!" replied the landlord, gazing at the dark features of his companion, where hardship, peril, and dissipation had each left their traces. "No, you are not like the slender boy of fifteen, who stood on the hill by moonlight to take a last look at his father's cottage. There were tears in your eyes then; and, as often as I remember them, I repent that I did not turn you back, instead of leading you on."

"Tears, were there? Well, there have been few enough since," said his comrade, pressing his eyelids firmly together, as if even then tempted to give way to the weakness that he scorned. "And, for turning me back, Hugh, it was beyond your power. I had taken my resolution, and you did but show me the way to execute it."

"You have not inquired after those you left behind," observed Hugh Crombie.

"No—no; nor will I have aught of them," exclaimed the traveller, starting from his seat, and pacing rapidly across the room. "My father, I know, is dead, and I have forgiven him. My mother—what could I hear of her but misery? I will hear nothing."

"You must have passed the cottage as you rode hitherward," said Hugh. "How could you forbear to enter?"

"I did not see it," he replied. "I closed my eyes, and turned away my head."

"Oh, if I had had a mother, a loving mother! if there had been one being in the world that loved me, or cared for me, I should not have become an utter castaway," exclaimed Hugh Crombie.

The landlord's pathos, like all pathos that flows from the winecup, was sufficiently ridiculous; and his companion, who had already overcome his own brief feelings of sorrow and remorse, now laughed aloud.

"Come, come, mine host of the Hand and Bottle," he cried in his usual hard, sarcastic tone; "be a man as much as in you lies. You had always a foolish trick of repentance; but, as I remember, it was commonly of a morning, before you had swallowed your first dram. And now, Hugh, fill the quart pot again, and we will to business."

When the landlord had complied with the wishes of his guest, the latter resumed in a lower tone than that of his ordinary conversation,—"There is a young lady lately become a resident hereabouts. Perhaps you can guess her name; for you have a quick apprehension in these matters."

"A young lady?" repeated Hugh Crombie. "And what is your concern with her? Do you mean Ellen Langton, daughter of the old merchant Langton, whom you have some cause to remember?"

"I do remember him; but he is where he will speedily be forgotten," answered the traveller. "And this girl,—I know your eye has been upon her, Hugh,—describe her to me."

"Describe her!" exclaimed Hugh with much animation. "It is impossible in prose; but you shall have her very picture in a verse of one of my own songs."

"Nay, mine host, I beseech you to spare me. This is no time for quavering," said the guest. "However, I am proud of your approbation, my old friend; for this young lady do I intend to take to wife. What think you of the plan?"

Hugh Crombie gazed into his companion's face for the space of a moment, in silence. There was nothing in its expression that looked like a jest. It still retained the same hard, cold look, that, except when Hugh had alluded to his home and family, it had worn through their whole conversation.

"On my word, comrade!" he at length replied, "my advice is, that you give over your application to the quart pot, and refresh your brain by a short nap. And yet your eye is cool and steady. What is the meaning of this?"

"Listen, and you shall know," said the guest. "The old man, her father, is in his grave."

"Not a bloody grave, I trust," interrupted the landlord, starting, and looking fearfully into his comrade's face.

"No, a watery one," he replied calmly. "You see, Hugh, I am a better man than you took me for. The old man's blood is not on my head, though my wrongs are on his. Now listen: he had no heir but this only daughter; and to her, and to the man she marries, all his wealth will belong. She shall marry me. Think you her father will rest easy in the ocean, Hugh Crombie, when I am his son-in-law?"

"No, he will rise up to prevent it, if need be," answered the landlord. "But the dead need not interpose to frustrate so wild a scheme."

"I understand you," said his comrade. "You are of opinion that the young lady's consent may not be so soon won as asked. Fear not for that, mine host. I have a winning way with me, when opportunity serves; and it shall serve with Ellen Langton. I will have no rivals in my wooing."

"Your intention, if I take it rightly, is to get this poor girl into your power, and then to force her into a marriage," said Hugh Crombie.

"It is; and I think I possess the means of doing it," replied his comrade. "But methinks, friend Hugh, my enterprise has not your good wishes."

"No; and I pray you to give it over," said Hugh Crombie, very earnestly. "The girl is young, lovely, and as good as she is fair. I cannot aid in her ruin. Nay, more: I must prevent it."

"Prevent it!" exclaimed the traveller, with a darkening countenance. "Think twice before you stir in this matter, I advise you. Ruin, do you say? Does a girl call it ruin to be made an honest wedded wife? No, no, mine host! nor does a widow either, else have you much to answer for."

"I gave the Widow Hutchins fair play, at least, which is more than poor Ellen is like to get," observed the landlord. "My old comrade, will you not give up this scheme?"

"My old comrade, I will not give up this scheme," returned the other, composedly. "Why, Hugh, what has come over you since we last met? Have we not done twenty worse deeds of a morning, and laughed over them at night?"

"He is right there," said Hugh Crombie, in a meditative tone. "Of a certainty, my conscience has grown unreasonably tender within the last two years. This one small sin, if I were to aid in it, would add but a trifle to the sum of mine. But then the poor girl!"

His companion overheard him thus communing with himself, and having had much former experience of his infirmity of purpose, doubted not that he should bend him to his will.

In fact, his arguments were so effectual, that Hugh at length, though reluctantly, promised his cooperation. It was necessary that their motions should be speedy; for on the second day thereafter, the arrival of the post would bring intelligence of the shipwreck by which Mr. Langton had perished.

"And after the deed is done," said the landlord, "I beseech you never to cross my path again. There have been more wicked thoughts in my head within the last hour than for the whole two years that I have been an honest man."

"What a saint art thou become, Hugh!" said his comrade. "But fear not that we shall meet again. When I leave this valley, it will be to enter it no more."

"And there is little danger that any other who has known me will chance upon me here," observed Hugh Crombie. "Our trade was unfavorable to length of days, and I suppose most of our old comrades have arrived at the end of theirs."

"One whom you knew well is nearer to you than you think," answered the traveller; "for I did not travel hitherward entirely alone."

CHAPTER V

"A naughty night to swim in."

SHAKESPEARE.

THE evening of the day succeeding the adventure of the angler was dark and tempestuous. The rain descended almost in a continuous sheet; and occasional powerful gusts of wind drove it hard against the northeastern windows of Hugh Crombie's inn. But at least one apartment of the interior presented a scene of comfort and of apparent enjoyment, the more delightful from its contrast with the elemental fury that raged without. A fire, which the dullness of the evening, though a summer one, made necessary, was burning brightly on the hearth; and in front was placed a small round table, sustaining wine and glasses. One of the guests for whom these preparations had been made was Edward Walcott; the other was a shy, awkward young man, distinguished, by the union of classic and rural dress, as having but lately become a student of Harley College. He seemed little at his ease, probably from a consciousness that he was on forbidden ground, and that the wine, of which he nevertheless swallowed a larger share than his companion, was an unlawful draught.

In the catalogue of crimes provided against by the laws of Harley College, that of tavern-haunting was one of the principal. The secluded situation of the seminary, indeed, gave its scholars but a very limited choice of vices; and this was, therefore, the usual channel by which the wildness of youth discharged itself. Edward Walcott, though naturally temperate, had been not an unfrequent offender in this respect,

49

for which a superfluity both of time and money might plead some excuse. But, since his acquaintance with Ellen Langton, he had rarely entered Hugh Crombie's doors; and an interruption in that acquaintance was the cause of his present appearance there.

Edward's jealous pride had been considerably touched on Ellen's compliance with the request of the angler. He had, by degrees, imperceptible perhaps to himself, assumed the right of feeling displeased with her conduct; and she had, as imperceptibly, accustomed herself to consider what would be his wishes, and to act accordingly. He would, indeed, in no contingency have ventured an open remonstrance; and such a proceeding would have been attended by a result the reverse of what he desired. But there existed between them a silent compact (acknowledged perhaps by neither, but felt by both), according to which they had regulated the latter part of their intercourse. Their lips had yet spoken no word of love; but some of love's rights and privileges had been assumed on the one side, and at least not disallowed on the other.

Edward's penetration had been sufficiently quick to discover that there was a mystery about the angler, that there must have been a cause for the blush that rose so proudly on Ellen's cheek; and his Quixotism had been not a little mortified, because she did not immediately appeal to his protection. He had, however, paid his usual visit the next day at Dr. Melmoth's, expecting that, by a smile of more than common brightness, she would make amends to his wounded feelings; such having been her usual mode of reparation in the few instances of disagreement that had occurred between them. But he was disappointed. He found her cold, silent, and abstracted, inattentive when he spoke, and indisposed to speak herself. Her eye was sedulously averted from his; and the casual meeting of their glances only proved that there were feelings in her bosom which he did not share. He was unable to account for this change in her deportment; and, added to his previous conceptions of his wrongs, it produced an effect upon his rather hasty temper, that might have manifested itself violently, but for the presence of Mrs. Melmoth. He took his leave in very evident displeasure; but, just as he closed the door, he noticed an expression in Ellen's countenance, that, had they been alone, and had not he been quite so proud, would have drawn him down to her feet. Their eyes met, when, suddenly, there was a gush of tears into those of Ellen; and a deep sadness, almost despair, spread itself over her features. He paused a moment, and then went his way, equally unable to account for her coldness, or for her grief. He was well aware, however, that his situation in respect to her was unaccountably changed,—a conviction so disagreeable, that, but for a hope that is latent even in the despair of youthful hearts, he would have been sorely tempted to shoot himself.

The gloom of his thoughts—a mood of mind the more intolerable to him, because so unusual—had driven him to Hugh Crombie's inn in search of artificial excitement. But even the wine had no attractions; and his first glass stood now almost untouched before him, while he gazed in heavy thought into the glowing embers of the fire. His companion perceived his melancholy, and essayed to dispel it by a choice of such topics of conversation as he conceived would be most agreeable.

"There is a lady in the house," he observed. "I caught a glimpse of her in the passage as we came in. Did you see her, Edward?"

"A lady!" repeated Edward, carelessly. "What know you of ladies? No, I did not see her; but I will venture to say that it was Dame Crombie's self, and no other."

"Well, perhaps it might," said the other, doubtingly. "Her head was turned from me, and she was gone like a shadow."

"Dame Crombie is no shadow, and never vanishes like one," resumed Edward. "You have mistaken the slipshod servant-girl for a lady."

"Ay; but she had a white hand, a small white hand," said the student, piqued at Edward's contemptuous opinion of his powers of observation; "as white as Ellen Langton's." He paused; for the lover was offended by the profanity of the comparison, as was made evident by the blood that rushed to his brow.

"We will appeal to the landlord," said Edward, recovering his equanimity, and turning to Hugh, who just then entered the room. "Who is this angel, mine host, that has taken up her abode in the Hand and Bottle?"

Hugh cast a quick glance from one to another before he answered, "I keep no angels here, gentlemen. Dame Crombie would make the house anything but heaven for them and me."

"And yet Glover has seen a vision in the passage-way,—a lady with a small white hand."

"Ah, I understand! A slight mistake of the young gentleman's," said Hugh, with the air of one who could perfectly account for the mystery. "Our passageway is dark; or perhaps the light had dazzled his eyes. It was the Widow Fowler's daughter, that came to borrow a pipe of tobacco for her mother. By the same token, she put it into her own sweet mouth, and puffed as she went along."

"But the white hand," said Glover, only half convinced.

"Nay, I know not," answered Hugh. "But her hand was at least as white as her face: that I can swear. Well, gentlemen, I trust you find everything in my house to your satisfaction. When the fire needs renewing, or the wine runs low, be pleased to tap on the table. I shall appear with the speed of a sunbeam."

After the departure of the landlord, the conversation of the young men amounted to little more than monosyllables. Edward Walcott was wrapped in his own contemplations; and his companion was in a half-slumberous state, from which he started every quarter of an hour, at the chiming of the clock that stood in a corner. The fire died gradually away; the lamps began to burn dim; and Glover, rousing himself from one of his periodical slumbers, was about to propose a return to their chambers. He was prevented, however, by the approach of footsteps along the passageway; and Hugh Crombie, opening the door, ushered a person into the room, and retired.

The new-comer was Fanshawe. The water that poured plentifully from his cloak evinced that he had but just arrived at the inn; but, whatever was his object, he seemed not to have attained it in meeting with the young men. He paused near the door, as if meditating whether to retire.

"My intrusion is altogether owing to a mistake, either of the landlord's or mine," he said. "I came hither to seek another person; but, as I could not mention his name, my inquiries were rather vague."

"I thank Heaven for the chance that sent you to us," replied Edward, rousing himself. "Glover is wretched company; and a duller evening have I never spent. We will renew our fire and our wine, and you must sit down with us. And for the man you seek," he continued in a whisper, "he left the inn within a half-hour after we encountered him. I inquired of Hugh Crombie last night."

Fanshawe did not express his doubts of the correctness of the information on which Edward seemed to rely. Laying aside his cloak, he accepted his invitation to make one of the party, and sat down by the fireside.

The aspect of the evening now gradually changed. A strange wild glee spread from one to another of the party, which, much to the surprise of his companions, began with and was communicated from, Fanshawe. He seemed to overflow with conceptions inimitably ludicrous, but so singular, that, till his hearers had imbibed a portion of his own spirit, they could only wonder at, instead of enjoying them. His applications to the wine were very unfrequent; yet his conversation was such as one might expect from a bottle of champagne endowed by a fairy with the gift of speech. The secret of this strange mirth lay in the troubled state of his spirits, which, like the vexed ocean at midnight (if the simile be not too magnificent), tossed forth a mysterious brightness. The undefined apprehensions that had drawn him to the inn still distracted his mind; but, mixed with them, there was a sort of joy not easily to be described. By degrees, and by the assistance of the wine, the inspiration spread, each one contributing such a quantity, and such quality of wit and whim, as was proportioned to his genius; but each one, and all, displaying a greater share of both than they had ever been suspected of possessing.

At length, however, there was a pause,—the deep pause of flagging spirits, that always follows mirth and wine. No one would have believed, on beholding the pensive faces, and hearing the involuntary sighs of the party, that from these, but a moment before, had arisen so loud and wild a laugh. During this interval Edward Walcott (who was the poet of his class) volunteered the following song, which, from its want of polish, and from its application to his present feelings, might charitably be taken for an extemporaneous production:—

The wine is bright, the wine is bright;
  And gay the drinkers be:
Of all that drain the bowl to-night,
  Most jollily drain we.
Oh, could one search the weary earth,—
  The earth from sea to sea,—
He'd turn and mingle in our mirth;
  For we're the merriest three.

Yet there are cares, oh, heavy cares!
  We know that they are nigh:
When forth each lonely drinker fares,
  Mark then his altered eye.
Care comes upon us when the jest
  And frantic laughter die;
And care will watch the parting guest—
  Oh late, then let us fly!

Hugh Crombie, whose early love of song and minstrelsy was still alive, had entered the room at the sound of Edward's voice, in sufficient time to accompany the second stanza on the violin. He now, with the air of one who was entitled to judge in these matters, expressed his opinion of the performance.

"Really, Master Walcott, I was not prepared for this," he said in the tone of condescending praise that a great man uses to his inferior when he chooses to overwhelm him with excess of joy. "Very well, indeed, young gentleman! Some of the lines, it is true, seem to have been dragged in by the head and shoulders; but I could scarcely have done much better myself at your age. With practice, and with such instruction as I might afford you, I should have little doubt of your becoming a distinguished poet. A great defect in your seminary, gentlemen,—the want of due cultivation in this heavenly art."

"Perhaps, sir," said Edward, with much gravity, "you might yourself be prevailed upon to accept the professorship of poetry?"

"Why, such an offer would require consideration," replied the landlord. "Professor Hugh Crombie of Harley College: it has a good sound, assuredly. But I am a public man, Master Walcott; and the public would be loath to spare me from my present office."

"Will Professor Crombie favor us with a specimen of his productions?" inquired Edward.

"Ahem, I shall be happy to gratify you, young gentleman," answered Hugh. "It is seldom, in this rude country, Master Walcott, that we meet with kindred genius; and the opportunity should never be thrown away."

Thus saying, he took a heavy draught of the liquor by which he was usually inspired, and the praises of which were the prevailing subject of his song; then, after much hemming, thrumming, and prelusion, and with many queer gestures and gesticulations, he began to effuse a lyric in the following fashion:—

I've been a jolly drinker this five-and-twenty year,
And still a jolly drinker, my friends, you see me here:
I sing the joys of drinking; bear a chorus, every man,
With pint pot and quart pot and clattering of can.

The sense of the professor's first stanza was not in exact proportion to the sound; but, being executed with great spirit, it attracted universal applause. This Hugh appropriated with a condescending bow and smile; and, making a signal for silence, he went on,—

King Solomon of old, boys (a jolly king was he),—

But here he was interrupted by a clapping of hands, that seemed a continuance of the applause bestowed on his former stanza. Hugh Crombie, who, as is the custom of many great performers, usually sang with his eyes shut, now opened them, intending gently to rebuke his auditors for their unseasonable expression of delight. He immediately perceived, however, that the fault was to be attributed to neither of the three young men; and, following the direction of their eyes, he saw near the door, in the dim background of the apartment, a figure in a cloak. The hat was flapped forward, the cloak muffled round the lower part of the face; and only the eyes were visible.

The party gazed a moment in silence, and then rushed *en masse* upon the intruder, the landlord bringing up the rear, and sounding a charge upon his fiddle. But, as they drew nigh, the black cloak began to assume a familiar look; the hat, also, was an old acquaintance; and, these being removed, from beneath them shone forth the reverend face and form of Dr. Melmoth. The president, in his quality of clergyman, had, late in the preceding afternoon, been called to visit an aged female who was supposed to be at the point of death. Her habitation was at the distance of several miles from Harley College; so that it was nightfall before Dr. Melmoth stood at her bedside. His stay had been lengthened beyond his anticipation, on account of the frame of mind in which he found the dying woman; and, after essaying to impart the comforts of religion to her disturbed intellect, he had waited for the abatement of the storm that had arisen while he was thus engaged. As the evening advanced, however, the rain poured down in undiminished cataracts; and the doctor, trusting to the prudence and sure-footedness of his steed, had at length set forth on his return. The darkness of the night, and the roughness of the road, might have appalled him, even had his horsemanship and his courage been more considerable than they were; but by the special protection of Providence, as he reasonably supposed (for he was a good man, and on a good errand), he arrived safely as far as Hugh Crombie's inn. Dr. Melmoth had no intention of making a stay there; but, as the road passed within a very short distance, he saw lights in the windows, and heard the sound of song and revelry. It immediately occurred to him, that these midnight rioters were, probably, some of the young men of his charge; and he was impelled, by a sense of duty, to enter and disperse them. Directed by the voices, he found his way, with some difficulty, to the apartment, just as Hugh concluded his first stanza; and, amidst the subsequent applause, his entrance had been un-perceived.

There was a silence of a moment's continuance after the discovery of Dr. Melmoth, during which he attempted to clothe his round, good-natured face in a look of awful dignity. But, in spite of himself, there was a little twisting of the corners of his mouth, and a smothered gleam in his eye.

"This has, apparently, been a very merry meeting, young gentlemen," he at length said; "but I fear my presence has cast a damp upon it."

"Oh yes! your reverence's cloak is wet enough to cast a damp upon anything," exclaimed Hugh Crombie, assuming a look of tender anxiety. "The young gentlemen are affrighted for your valuable life. Fear deprives them of utterance: permit me to relieve you of these dangerous garments."

"Trouble not yourself, honest man," replied the doctor, who was one of the most gullible of mortals. "I trust I am in no danger; my dwelling being near at hand. But for these young men"—

"Would your reverence but honor my Sunday suit,—the gray broadcloth coat, and the black velvet smallclothes, that have covered my unworthy legs but once? Dame Crombie shall have them ready in a moment," continued Hugh, beginning to divest the doctor of his garments.

"I pray you to appease your anxiety," cried Dr. Melmoth, retaining a firm hold on such parts of his dress as yet remained to him. "Fear not for my health. I will but speak a word to those misguided youth, and be gone."

"Misguided youth, did your reverence say?" echoed Hugh, in a tone of utter astonishment. "Never were they better guided than when they entered my poor house. Oh, had your reverence but seen them, when I heard their cries, and rushed forth to their assistance. Dripping with wet were they, like three drowned men at the resurrec—Ahem!" interrupted Hugh, recollecting that the comparison he meditated might not suit the doctor's ideas of propriety.

"But why were they abroad on such a night?" inquired the president.

"Ah! doctor, you little know the love these good young gentlemen bear for you," replied the landlord. "Your absence, your long absence, had alarmed them; and they rushed forth through the rain and darkness to seek you."

"And was this indeed so?" asked the doctor, in a softened tone, and casting a tender and grateful look upon the three students. They, it is but justice to mention, had simultaneously made a step forward in order to contradict the egregious falsehoods of which Hugh's fancy was so fertile; but he assumed an expression of such ludicrous entreaty, that it was irresistible.

"But methinks their anxiety was not of long continuance," observed Dr. Melmoth, looking at the wine, and remembering the song that his entrance had interrupted.

"Ah! your reverence disapproves of the wine, I see," answered Hugh Crombie. "I did but offer them a drop to keep the life in their poor young hearts. My dame advised strong waters; 'But, Dame Crombie,' says I, 'would ye corrupt their youth?' And in my zeal for their good, doctor, I was delighting them, just at your entrance, with a pious little melody of my own against the sin of drunkenness."

"Truly, I remember something of the kind," observed Dr. Melmoth. "And, as I think, it seemed to meet with good acceptance."

"Ay, that it did!" said the landlord. "Will it please your reverence to hear it?—

King Solomon of old, boys (a wise man I'm thinking),
Has warned you to beware of the horrid vice of drinking—

"But why talk I of drinking, foolish man that I am! And all this time, doctor, you have not sipped a drop of my wine. Now I entreat your reverence, as you value your health and the peace and quiet of these youth."

Dr. Melmoth drank a glass of wine, with the benevolent intention of allaying the anxiety of Hugh Crombie and the students. He then prepared to depart; for a strong wind had partially dispersed the clouds, and occasioned an interval in the cataract of rain. There was, perhaps, a little suspicion yet remaining in the good man's mind respecting the truth of the landlord's story: at least, it was his evident intention to see the students fairly out of the inn before he quitted it himself. They therefore proceeded along the passageway in a body. The lamp that Hugh Crombie held but dimly enlightened them; and the number and contiguity of the doors caused Dr. Melmoth to lay his hand upon the wrong one.

"Not there, not there, doctor! It is Dame Crombie's bedchamber," shouted Hugh, most energetically. "Now Beelzebub defend me!" he muttered to himself, perceiving that his exclamation had been a moment too late.

"Heavens! what do I see?" ejaculated Dr. Melmoth, lifting his hands, and starting back from the entrance of the room. The three students pressed forward; Mrs. Crombie and the servant-girl had been drawn to the spot by the sound of Hugh's voice; and all their wondering eyes were fixed on poor Ellen Langton.

The apartment in the midst of which she stood was dimly lighted by a solitary candle at the farther extremity; but Ellen was exposed to the glare of the three lamps, held by Hugh, his wife, and the servant-girl. Their combined rays seemed to form a focus exactly at the point where they reached her; and the beholders, had any been sufficiently calm, might have watched her features in their agitated workings and frequent change of expression, as perfectly as by the broad light of day. Terror had at first blanched her as white as a lily, or as a marble statue, which for a moment she resembled, as she stood motionless in the centre of the room. Shame next bore sway; and her blushing countenance, covered by her slender white fingers, might fantastically be compared to a variegated rose with its alternate stripes of white and red. The next instant, a sense of her pure and innocent intentions gave her strength and courage; and her attitude and look had now something of pride and dignity. These, however, in their turn, gave way; for Edward Walcott pressed forward, and attempted to address her.

"Ellen, Ellen!" he said, in an agitated and quivering whisper; but what was to follow cannot be known; for his emotion checked his utterance. His tone and look, however, again overcame Ellen Langton, and she burst into tears. Fanshawe advanced, and took Edward's arm. "She has been deceived," he whispered. "She is innocent: you are unworthy of her if you doubt it."

"Why do you interfere, sir?" demanded Edward, whose passions, thoroughly excited, would willingly have wreaked themselves on any one. "What right have you to speak of her innocence? Perhaps," he continued, an undefined and ridiculous suspicion arising in his mind,—"perhaps you are acquainted with her intentions. Perhaps you are the deceiver."

Fanshawe's temper was not naturally of the meekest character; and having had a thousand bitter feelings of his own to overcome, before he could attempt to console Edward, this rude repulse had almost aroused him to fierceness. But his pride, of which a more moderate degree would have had a less peaceable effect, came to his assistance; and he turned calmly and contemptuously away.

Ellen, in the mean time, had been restored to some degree of composure. To this effect, a feeling of pique against Edward Walcott had contributed. She had distinguished his voice in the neighboring apartment, had heard his mirth and wild laughter, without being aware of the state of feeling that produced them. She had supposed that the terms on which they parted in the morning (which had been very grievous to herself) would have produced a corresponding sadness in him. But while she sat in loneliness and in tears, her bosom distracted by a thousand anxieties and sorrows, of many of which Edward was the object, his reckless gayety had seemed to prove the slight regard in which he held her. After the first outbreak of emotion, therefore, she called up her pride (of which, on proper occasions, she had a reasonable share), and sustained his upbraiding glance with a passive composure, which women have more readily at command than men.

Dr. Melmoth's surprise had during this time kept him silent and inactive. He gazed alternately from one to another of those who stood around him, as if to seek some explanation of so strange an event. But the faces of all were as perplexed as his own; even Hugh Crombie had assumed a look of speechless wonder,—speechless, because his imagination, prolific as it was, could not supply a plausible falsehood.

"Ellen, dearest child," at length said the doctor, "what is the meaning of this?"

Ellen endeavored to reply; but, as her composure was merely external, she was unable to render her words audible. Fanshawe spoke in a low voice to Dr. Melmoth, who appeared grateful for his advice.

"True, it will be the better way," he replied. "My wits are utterly confounded, or I should not have remained thus long. Come, my dear child," he continued, advancing to Ellen, and taking her hand, "let us return home, and defer the explanation till the morrow. There, there: only dry your eyes, and we will say no more about it."

"And that will be your wisest way, old gentleman," muttered Hugh Crombie.

Ellen at first exhibited but little desire, or, rather, an evident reluctance, to accompany her guardian. She hung back, while her glance passed almost imperceptibly over the faces that gazed so eagerly at her; but the one she sought was not visible among them. She had no alternative, and suffered herself to be led from the inn.

Edward Walcott alone remained behind, the most wretched being (at least such was his own opinion) that breathed the vital air. He felt a sinking and sickness of the heart, and alternately a feverish frenzy, neither of which his short and cloudless existence had heretofore occasioned him to experience. He was jealous of, he knew not whom, and he knew not what. He was ungenerous enough to believe that Ellen—his pure and lovely Ellen—had degraded herself; though from what motive, or by whose agency, he could not conjecture. When Dr. Melmoth had taken her in charge, Edward returned to the apartment where he had spent the evening. The wine was still upon the table; and, in the desperate hope of stupefying his faculties, he unwisely swallowed huge successive draughts. The effect of his imprudence was not long in manifesting itself; though insensibility, which at another time would have been the result, did not now follow. Acting upon his previous agitation, the wine seemed to set his blood in a flame; and, for the time being, he was a perfect madman.

A phrenologist would probably have found the organ of destructiveness in strong development, just then, upon Edward's cranium; for he certainly manifested an impulse to break and destroy whatever chanced to be within his reach. He commenced his operations by upsetting the table, and breaking the bottles and glasses. Then, seizing a tall heavy chair in each hand, he hurled them with prodigious force,—one through the window, and the other against a large looking-glass, the most valuable article of furniture in Hugh Crombie's inn. The crash and clatter of these outrageous proceedings soon brought the master, mistress, and maid-servant to the scene of action; but the two latter, at the first sight of Edward's wild demeanor and gleaming eyes, retreated with all imaginable expedition. Hugh chose a position behind the door, from whence, protruding his head, he endeavored to mollify his inebriated guest. His interference, however, had nearly been productive of most unfortunate consequences; for a massive andiron, with round brazen head, whizzed past him, within a hair's-breadth of his ear.

"I might as safely take my chance in a battle," exclaimed Hugh, withdrawing his head, and speaking to a man who stood in the passageway. "A little twist of his hand to the left would have served my turn as well as if I stood in the path of a forty-two pound ball. And here comes another broadside," he added, as some other article of furniture rattled against the door.

"Let us return his fire, Hugh," said the person whom he addressed, composedly lifting the andiron. "He is in want of ammunition: let us send him back his own."

The sound of this man's voice produced a most singular effect upon Edward. The moment before, his actions had been those of a raving maniac; but, when the words struck his ear, he paused, put his hand to his forehead, seemed to recollect himself, and finally advanced with a firm and steady step. His countenance was dark and angry, but no longer wild.

"I have found you, villain!" he said to the angler. "It is you who have done this."

"And, having done it, the wrath of a boy—his drunken wrath—will not induce me to deny it," replied the other, scornfully.

"The boy will require a man's satisfaction," returned Edward, "and that speedily."

"Will you take it now?" inquired the angler, with a cool, derisive smile, and almost in a whisper. At the same time he produced a brace of pistols, and held them towards the young man.

"Willingly," answered Edward, taking one of the weapons. "Choose your distance."

The angler stepped back a pace; but before their deadly intentions, so suddenly conceived, could be executed, Hugh Crombie interposed himself between them.

"Do you take my best parlor for the cabin of the Black Andrew, where a pistol-shot was a nightly pastime?" he inquired of his comrade. "And you, Master Edward, with what sort of a face will you walk into the chapel to morning prayers, after putting a ball through this man's head, or receiving one through your own? Though, in this last case, you will be past praying for, or praying either."

"Stand aside: I will take the risk. Make way, or I will put the ball through your own head," exclaimed Edward, fiercely: for the interval of rationality that circumstances had produced was again giving way to intoxication.

"You see how it is," said Hugh to his companion, unheard by Edward. "You shall take a shot at me, sooner than at the poor lad in his present state. You have done him harm enough already, and intend him more. I propose," he continued aloud, and with a peculiar glance towards the angler, "that this affair be decided to-morrow, at nine o'clock, under the old oak, on the bank of the stream. In the mean time, I will take charge of these popguns, for fear of accidents."

"Well, mine host, be it as you wish," said his comrade. "A shot more or less is of little consequence to me." He accordingly delivered his weapon to Hugh Crombie and walked carelessly away.

"Come, Master Walcott, the enemy has retreated. Victoria! And now, I see, the sooner I get you to your chamber, the better," added he aside; for the wine was at last beginning to produce its legitimate effect, in stupefying the young man's mental and bodily faculties.

Hugh Crombie's assistance, though not, perhaps, quite indispensable, was certainly very convenient to our unfortunate hero, in the course of the short walk that brought him to his chamber. When arrived there, and in bed, he was soon locked in a sleep scarcely less deep than that of death.

The weather, during the last hour, had appeared to be on the point of changing: indeed, there were, every few minutes, most rapid changes. A strong breeze sometimes drove the clouds from the brow of heaven, so as to disclose a few of the stars; but, immediately after, the darkness would again become Egyptian, and the rain rush like a torrent from the sky.

CHAPTER VI

"About her neck a packet-mail
Fraught with advice, some fresh, some stale,
Of men that walked when they were dead."

HUDIBRAS.

SCARCELY a word had passed between Dr. Melmoth and Ellen Langton, on their way home; for, though the former was aware that his duty towards his ward would compel him to inquire into the motives of her conduct, the tenderness of his heart prompted him to defer the scrutiny to the latest moment. The same tenderness induced him to connive at Ellen's stealing secretly up to her chamber, unseen by Mrs. Melmoth; to render which measure practicable, he opened the house-door very softly, and stood before his half-sleeping spouse (who waited his arrival in the parlor) without any previous notice. This act of the doctor's benevolence was not destitute of heroism; for he was well assured that, should the affair come to the lady's knowledge through any other channel, her vengeance would descend not less heavily on him for concealing, than on Ellen for perpetrating, the elopement. That she had, thus far, no suspicion of the fact, was evident from her composure, as well as from the reply to a question, which, with more than his usual art, her husband put to her respecting the non-appearance of his ward. Mrs. Melmoth answered, that Ellen had complained of indisposition, and after drinking, by her prescription, a large cup of herb-tea, had retired to her chamber early in the evening. Thankful that all was yet safe, the doctor laid his head upon his pillow;

but, late as was the hour, his many anxious thoughts long drove sleep from his eyelids.

The diminution in the quantity of his natural rest did not, however, prevent Dr. Melmoth from rising at his usual hour, which at all seasons of the year was an early one. He found, on descending to the parlor, that breakfast was nearly in readiness; for the lady of the house (and, as a corollary, her servant-girl) was not accustomed to await the rising of the sun in order to commence her domestic labors. Ellen Langton, however, who had heretofore assimilated her habits to those of the family, was this morning invisible,—a circumstance imputed by Mrs. Melmoth to her indisposition of the preceding evening, and by the doctor, to mortification on account of her elopement and its discovery.

"I think I will step into Ellen's bedchamber," said Mrs. Melmoth, "and inquire how she feels herself. The morning is delightful after the storm, and the air will do her good."

"Had we not better proceed with our breakfast? If the poor child is sleeping, it were a pity to disturb her," observed the doctor; for, besides his sympathy with Ellen's feelings, he was reluctant, as if he were the guilty one, to meet her face.

"Well, be it so. And now sit down, doctor; for the hot cakes are cooling fast. I suppose you will say they are not so good as those Ellen made yesterday morning. I know not how you will bear to part with her, though the thing must soon be."

"It will be a sore trial, doubtless," replied Dr. Melmoth,— "like tearing away a branch that is grafted on an old tree. And yet there will be a satisfaction in delivering her safe into her father's hands."

"A satisfaction for which you may thank me, doctor," observed the lady. "If there had been none but you to look after the poor thing's doings, she would have been enticed away long ere this, for the sake of her money."

Dr. Melmoth's prudence could scarcely restrain a smile at the thought that an elopement, as he had reason to believe, had been plotted, and partly carried into execution, while Ellen was under the sole care of his lady, and had been frustrated only by his own despised agency. He was not accustomed, however,—nor was this an eligible occasion,—to dispute any of Mrs. Melmoth's claims to superior wisdom.

The breakfast proceeded in silence, or, at least, without any conversation material to the tale. At its conclusion, Mrs. Melmoth was again meditating on the propriety of entering Ellen's chamber; but she was now prevented by an incident that always excited much interest both in herself and her husband.

This was the entrance of the servant, bearing the letters and newspaper, with which, once a fortnight, the mail-carrier journeyed up the valley. Dr. Melmoth's situation at the head of a respectable seminary, and his character as a scholar, had procured him an extensive correspondence among the learned men of his own country; and he had even exchanged epistles with one or two of the most distinguished dissenting clergymen of Great Britain. But, unless when some fond mother enclosed a one-pound note to defray the private expenses of her son at college, it was frequently the case that the packets addressed to the doctor were the sole contents of the mail-bag. In the present instance, his letters were very numerous, and, to judge from the one he chanced first to open, of an unconscionable length. While he was engaged in their perusal, Mrs. Melmoth amused herself with the newspaper,—a little sheet of about twelve inches square, which had but one rival in the country. Commencing with the title, she labored on through advertisements old and new, through poetry lamentably deficient in rhythm and rhymes, through essays, the ideas of which had been trite since the first week of the creation, till she finally arrived at the department that, a fortnight before, had contained the latest news from all quarters. Making such remarks upon these items as to her seemed good, the dame's notice was at length attracted by an article which her sudden exclamation proved to possess uncommon interest. Casting her eye hastily over it, she immediately began to read aloud to her husband; but he, deeply engaged in a long and learned letter, instead of listening to what she wished to communicate, exerted his own lungs in opposition to hers, as is the custom of abstracted men when disturbed. The result was as follows:—

"A brig just arrived in the outer harbor," began Mrs. Melmoth, "reports, that on the morning of the 25th ult."—Here the doctor broke in, "Wherefore I am compelled to differ from your exposition of the said passage, for those reasons, of the which I have given you a taste; provided"—The lady's voice was now almost audible, "ship bottom upward, discovered by the name on her stern to be the Ellen of"—"and in the same opinion are Hooker, Cotton, and divers learned divines of a later date."

The doctor's lungs were deep and strong, and victory seemed to incline toward him; but Mrs. Melmoth now made use of a tone whose peculiar shrillness, as long experience had taught her husband, augured a mood of mind not to be trifled with.

"On my word, doctor," she exclaimed, "this is most unfeeling and unchristian conduct! Here am I endeavoring to inform you of the death of an old friend, and you continue as deaf as a post."

Dr. Melmoth, who had heard the sound, without receiving the sense, of these words, now laid aside the letter in despair, and submissively requested to be informed of her pleasure.

"There, read for yourself," she replied, handing him the paper, and pointing to the passage containing the important intelligence,—"read, and then finish your letter, if you have a mind."

He took the paper, unable to conjecture how the dame could be so much interested in any part of its contents; but, before he had read many words, he grew pale as death. "Good Heavens! what is this?" he exclaimed. He then read on, "being the vessel wherein that eminent son of New England, John Langton, Esq., had taken passage for his native country, after an absence of many years."

"Our poor Ellen, his orphan child!" said Dr. Melmoth, dropping the paper. "How shall we break the intelligence to her? Alas! her share of the affliction causes me to forget my own."

"It is a heavy misfortune, doubtless; and Ellen will grieve as a daughter should," replied Mrs. Melmoth, speaking with the good sense of which she had a competent share. "But she has never known her father; and her sorrow must arise from a sense of duty, more than from strong affection. I will go and inform her of her loss. It is late, and I wonder if she be still asleep."

"Be cautious, dearest wife," said the doctor. "Ellen has strong feelings, and a sudden shock might be dangerous."

"I think I may be trusted, Dr. Melmoth," replied the lady, who had a high opinion of her own abilities as a comforter, and was not averse to exercise them.

Her husband, after her departure, sat listlessly turning over the letters that yet remained unopened, feeling little curiosity, after such melancholy intelligence, respecting their contents. But, by the handwriting of the direction on one of them, his attention was gradually arrested, till he found himself gazing earnestly on those strong, firm, regular characters. They were perfectly familiar to his eye; but from what hand they came, he could not conjecture. Suddenly, however, the truth burst upon him; and after noticing the date, and reading a few lines, he rushed hastily in pursuit of his wife.

He had arrived at the top of his speed and at the middle of the staircase, when his course was arrested by the lady whom he sought, who came, with a velocity equal to his own, in an opposite direction. The consequence was a concussion between the two meeting masses, by which Mrs. Melmoth was seated securely on the stairs; while the doctor was only preserved from precipitation to the bottom by clinging desperately to the balustrade. As soon as the pair discovered that they had sustained no material injury by their contact, they began eagerly to explain the cause of their mutual haste, without those reproaches, which, on the lady's part, would at another time have followed such an accident.

"You have not told her the bad news, I trust?" cried Dr. Melmoth, after each had communicated his and her intelligence, without obtaining audience of the other.

"Would you have me tell it to the bare walls?" inquired the lady in her shrillest tone. "Have I not just informed you that she has gone, fled, eloped? Her chamber is empty; and her bed has not been occupied."

"Gone!" repeated the doctor. "And, when her father comes to demand his daughter of me, what answer shall I make?"

"Now, Heaven defend us from the visits of the dead and drowned!" cried Mrs. Melmoth. "This is a serious affair, doctor, but not, I trust, sufficient to raise a ghost."

"Mr. Langton is yet no ghost," answered he; "though this event will go near to make him one. He was fortunately prevented, after he had made every preparation, from taking passage in the vessel that was lost."

"And where is he now?" she inquired.

"He is in New England. Perhaps he is at this moment on his way to us," replied her husband. "His letter is dated nearly a fortnight back; and he expresses an intention of being with us in a few days."

"Well, I thank Heaven for his safety," said Mrs. Melmoth. "But truly the poor gentleman could not have chosen a better time to be drowned, nor a worse one to come to life, than this. What we shall do, doctor, I know not; but had you locked the doors, and fastened the windows, as I advised, the misfortune could not have happened."

"Why, the whole country would have flouted us!" answered the doctor. "Is there a door in all the Province that is barred or bolted, night or day? Nevertheless it might have been advisable last night, had it occurred to me."

"And why at that time more than at all times?" she inquired. "We had surely no reason to fear this event."

Dr. Melmoth was silent; for his worldly wisdom was sufficient to deter him from giving his lady the opportunity, which she would not fail to use to the utmost, of laying the blame of the elopement at his door. He now proceeded, with a heavy heart, to Ellen's chamber, to satisfy himself with his own eyes of the state of affairs. It was deserted too truly; and the wildflowers with which it was the maiden's custom daily to decorate her premises were drooping, as if in sorrow for her who had placed them there. Mrs. Melmoth, on this second visit, discovered on the table a note addressed to her husband, and containing a few words of gratitude from Ellen, but no explanation of her mysterious flight. The doctor gazed long on the tiny letters, which had evidently been traced with a trembling hand, and blotted with many tears.

"There is a mystery in this,—a mystery that I cannot fathom," he said. "And now I would I knew what measures it would be proper to take."

"Get you on horseback, Dr. Melmoth, and proceed as speedily as may be down the valley to the town," said the dame, the influence of whose firmer mind was sometimes, as in the present case, most beneficially exerted over his own. "You must not spare for trouble, no, nor for danger. Now—Oh, if I were a man!"—

"Oh, that you were!" murmured the doctor, in a perfectly inaudible voice, "Well—and when I reach the town, what then?"

"As I am a Christian woman, my patience cannot endure you!" exclaimed Mrs. Melmoth. "Oh, I love to see a man with the spirit of a man! but you"—And she turned away in utter scorn.

"But, dearest wife," remonstrated the husband, who was really at a loss how to proceed, and anxious for her advice, "your worldly experience is greater than mine, and I desire to profit by it. What should be my next measure after arriving at the town?"

Mrs. Melmoth was appeased by the submission with which the doctor asked her counsel; though, if the truth must be told, she heartily despised him for needing it. She condescended, however, to instruct him in the proper method of pursuing the runaway maiden, and directed him, before his departure, to put strict inquiries to Hugh Crombie respecting any stranger who might lately have visited his inn. That there would be wisdom in this, Dr. Melmoth had his own reasons for believing; and still, without imparting them to his lady, he proceeded to do as he had been bid.

The veracious landlord acknowledged that a stranger had spent a night and day at his inn, and was missing that morning; but he utterly denied all acquaintance with his character, or privity to his purposes. Had Mrs. Melmoth, instead of her husband, conducted the examination, the result might have been different. As the case was, the doctor returned to his dwelling but little wiser than he went forth; and, ordering his steed to be saddled, he began a journey of which he knew not what would be the end.

In the mean time, the intelligence of Ellen's disappearance circulated rapidly, and soon sent forth hunters more fit to follow the chase than Dr. Melmoth.

CHAPTER VII

"There was racing and chasing o'er Cannobie Lee."

WALTER SCOTT.

WHEN Edward Walcott awoke the next morning from his deep slumber, his first consciousness was of a heavy weight upon his mind, the cause of which he was unable immediately to recollect. One by one, however, by means of the association of ideas, the events of the preceding night came back to his memory; though those of latest occurrence were dim as dreams. But one circumstance was only too well remembered,—the discovery of Ellen Langton. By a strong effort he next attained to an uncertain recollection of a scene of madness and violence, followed, as he at first thought, by a duel. A little further reflection, however, informed him that this event was yet among the things of futurity; but he could by no means recall the appointed time or place. As he had not the slightest intention (praiseworthy and prudent as it would unquestionably have been) to give up the chance of avenging Ellen's wrongs and his own, he immediately arose, and began to dress, meaning to learn from Hugh Crombie those particulars which his own memory had not retained. His chief apprehension was, that the appointed time had already elapsed; for the early Sunbeams of a glorious morning were now peeping into his chamber.

More than once, during the progress of dressing, he was inclined to believe that the duel had actually taken place, and been fatal to him, and that he was now in those regions to which, his conscience told him, such an event would be likely to send him. This idea resulted from his bodily sensations, which were in the highest degree uncomfortable. He was tormented by a raging thirst, that seemed to have absorbed all the moisture of his throat and stomach; and, in his present agitation, a cup of icy water would have been his first wish, had all the treasures of earth and sea been at his command. His head, too, throbbed almost to bursting; and the whirl of his brain at every movement promised little accuracy in the aim of his pistol, when he should meet the angler. These feelings, together with the deep degradation of his mind, made him resolve that no circumstances should again draw him into an excess of wine. In the mean time, his head was, perhaps, still too much confused to allow him fully to realize his unpleasant situation.

Before Edward was prepared to leave his chamber, the door was opened by one of the college bed-makers, who, perceiving that he was nearly dressed, entered, and began to set the apartment in order. There were two of these officials pertaining to Harley College; each of them being (and, for obvious reasons, this was an indispensable qualification) a model of perfect ugliness in her own way. One was a tall, raw-boned, huge-jointed, double-fisted giantess, admirably fitted to sustain the part of Glumdalia, in the tragedy of "Tom Thumb." Her features were as excellent as her form, appearing to have been rough-hewn with a broadaxe, and left unpolished. The other was a short, squat figure, about two thirds the height, and three times the circumference, of ordinary females. Her hair was gray, her complexion of a deep yellow; and her most remarkable feature was a short snub nose, just discernible amid the broad immensity of her face. This latter lady was she who now entered Edward's chamber. Notwithstanding her deficiency in personal attractions, she was rather a favorite of the students, being good-natured, anxious for their comfort, and, when duly encouraged, very communicative. Edward perceived, as soon as she appeared, that she only waited his assistance in order to disburden herself of some extraordinary information; and, more from compassion than curiosity, he began to question her.

"Well, Dolly, what news this morning?"

"Why, let me see,—oh, yes! It had almost slipped my memory," replied the bed-maker. "Poor Widow Butler died last night, after her long sickness. Poor woman! I remember her forty years ago, or so,—as rosy a lass as you could set eyes on."

"Ah! has she gone?" said Edward, recollecting the sick woman of the cottage which he had entered with Ellen and Fanshawe. "Was she not out of her right mind, Dolly?"

"Yes, this seven years," she answered. "They say she came to her senses a bit, when Dr. Melmoth visited her yesterday, but was raving mad when she died. Ah, that son of hers!—if he is yet alive. Well, well!"

"She had a son, then?" inquired Edward.

"Yes, such as he was. The Lord preserve me from such a one!" said Dolly. "It was thought he went off with Hugh Crombie, that keeps the tavern now. That was fifteen years ago."

"And have they heard nothing of him since?" asked Edward.

"Nothing good,—nothing good," said the bed-maker.

"Stories did travel up the valley now and then; but for five years there has been no word of him. They say Merchant Langton, Ellen's father, met him in foreign parts, and would have made a man of him; but there was too much of the wicked one in him for that. Well, poor woman! I wonder who'll preach her funeral sermon."

"Dr. Melmoth, probably," observed the student.

"No, no! The doctor will never finish his journey in time. And who knows but his own funeral will be the end of it," said Dolly, with a sagacious shake of her head.

"Dr. Melmoth gone a journey!" repeated Edward. "What do you mean? For what purpose?"

"For a good purpose enough, I may say," replied she. "To search out Miss Ellen, that was run away with last night."

"In the Devil's name, woman, of what are you speaking?" shouted Edward, seizing the affrighted bed-maker forcibly by the arm.

Poor Dolly had chosen this circuitous method of communicating her intelligence, because she was well aware that, if she first told of Ellen's flight, she should find no ear for her account of the Widow Butler's death. She had not calculated, however, that the news would produce so violent an effect upon her auditor; and her voice faltered as she recounted what she knew of the affair. She had hardly concluded, before Edward—who, as she proceeded, had been making hasty preparations—rushed from his chamber, and took the way towards Hugh Crombie's inn. He had no difficulty in finding the landlord, who had already occupied his accustomed seat, and was smoking his accustomed pipe, under the elm-tree.

"Well, Master Walcott, you have come to take a stomach-reliever this morning, I suppose," said Hugh, taking the pipe from his mouth. "What shall it be?—a bumper of wine with an egg? or a glass of smooth, old, oily brandy, such as Dame Crombie and I keep for our own drinking? Come, that will do it, I know."

"No, no! neither," replied Edward, shuddering involuntarily at the bare mention of wine and strong drink. "You know well, Hugh Crombie, the errand on which I come."

"Well, perhaps I do," said the landlord. "You come to order me to saddle my best horse. You are for a ride, this fine morning."

"True; and I must learn of you in what direction to turn my horse's head," replied Edward Walcott.

"I understand you," said Hugh, nodding and smiling. "And now, Master Edward, I really have taken a strong liking to you; and, if you please to hearken to it, you shall have some of my best advice."

"Speak," said the young man, expecting to be told in what direction to pursue the chase.

"I advise you, then," continued Hugh Crombie, in a tone in which some real feeling mingled with assumed carelessness,—"I advise you to forget that you have ever known this girl, that she has ever existed; for she is as much lost to you as if she never had been born, or as if the grave had covered her. Come, come, man, toss off a quart of my old wine, and kept up a merry heart. This has been my way in many a heavier sorrow than ever you have felt; and you see I am alive and merry yet." But Hugh's merriment had failed him just as he was making his boast of it; for Edward saw a tear in the corner of his eye.

"Forget her? Never, never!" said the student, while his heart sank within him at the hopelessness of pursuit which Hugh's words implied. "I will follow her to the ends of the earth."

"Then so much the worse for you and for my poor nag, on whose back you shall be in three minutes," rejoined the landlord. "I have spoken to you as I would to my own son, if I had such an incumbrance.—Here, you ragamuffin; saddle the gray, and lead him round to the door."

"The gray? I will ride the black," said Edward. "I know your best horse as well as you do yourself, Hugh."

"There is no black horse in my stable. I have parted with him to an old comrade of mine," answered the landlord, with a wink of acknowledgment to what he saw were Edward's suspicions. "The gray is a stout nag, and will carry you a round pace, though not so fast as to bring you up with them you seek. I reserved him for you, and put Mr. Fanshawe off with the old white, on which I travelled hitherward a year or two since."

"Fanshawe! Has he, then, the start of me?" asked Edward.

"He rode off about twenty minutes ago," replied Hugh; "but you will overtake him within ten miles, at farthest. But, if mortal man could recover the girl, that fellow would do it, even if he had no better nag than a broomstick, like the witches of old times."

"Did he obtain any information from you as to the course?" inquired the student.

"I could give him only this much," said Hugh, pointing down the road in the direction of the town. "My old comrade trusts no man further than is needful, and I ask no unnecessary questions."

The hostler now led up to the door the horse which Edward was to ride. The young man mounted with all expedition; but, as he was about to apply the spurs, his thirst, which the bed-maker's intelligence had caused him to forget, returned most powerfully upon him.

"For Heaven's sake, Hugh, a mug of your sharpest cider; and let it be a large one!" he exclaimed. "My tongue rattles in my mouth like"—

"Like the bones in a dice-box," said the landlord, finishing the comparison, and hastening to obey Edward's directions. Indeed, he rather exceeded them, by mingling with the juice of the apple a gill of his old brandy, which his own experience told him would at that time have a most desirable effect upon the young man's internal system.

"It is powerful stuff, mine host; and I feel like a new man already," observed Edward, after draining the mug to the bottom.

"He is a fine lad, and sits his horse most gallantly," said Hugh Crombie to himself as the student rode off. "I heartily wish him success. I wish to Heaven my conscience had suffered me to betray the plot before it was too late. Well, well, a man must keep his mite of honesty."

The morning was now one of the most bright and glorious that ever shone for mortals; and, under other circumstances, Edward's bosom would have been as light, and his spirit would have sung as cheerfully, as one of the many birds that warbled around him. The raindrops of the preceding night hung like glittering diamonds on every leaf of every tree, shaken, and rendered more brilliant, by occasional sighs of wind, that removed from the traveller the superfluous heat of an unclouded sun. In spite of the adventure, so mysterious and vexatious, in which he was engaged, Edward's elastic spirit (assisted, perhaps, by the brandy he had unwittingly swallowed) rose higher as he rode on; and he soon found himself endeavoring to accommodate the tune of one of Hugh Crombie's ballads to the motion of the horse. Nor did this reviving cheerfulness argue anything against his unwavering faith, and pure and fervent love for Ellen Langton. A sorrowful and repining disposition is not the necessary accompaniment of a "leal and loving heart"; and Edward's spirits were cheered, not by forgetfulness, but by hope, which would not permit him to doubt of the ultimate success of his pursuit. The uncertainty itself, and the probable danger of the expedition, were not without their charm to a youthful and adventurous spirit. In fact, Edward would not have been altogether satisfied to recover the errant damsel, without first doing battle in her behalf.

He had proceeded but a few miles before he came in sight of Fanshawe, who had been accommodated by the landlord with a horse much inferior to his own. The speed to which he had been put had almost exhausted the poor animal, whose best pace was now but little beyond a walk. Edward drew his bridle as he came up with Fanshawe.

"I have been anxious to apologize," he said to him, "for the hasty and unjust expressions of which I made use last evening.

May I hope that, in consideration of my mental distraction and the causes of it, you will forget what has passed?"

"I had already forgotten it," replied Fanshawe, freely offering his hand. "I saw your disturbed state of feeling, and it would have been unjust both to you and to myself to remember the errors it occasioned."

"A wild expedition this," observed Edward, after shaking warmly the offered hand. "Unless we obtain some further information at the town, we shall hardly know which way to continue the pursuit."

"We can scarcely fail, I think, of lighting upon some trace of them," said Fanshawe. "Their flight must have commenced after the storm subsided, which would give them but a few hours the start of us. May I beg," he continued, nothing the superior condition of his rival's horse, "that you will not attempt to accommodate your pace to mine?"

Edward bowed, and rode on, wondering at the change which a few months had wrought in Fanshawe's character. On this occasion, especially, the energy of his mind had communicated itself to his frame. The color was strong and high in his cheek; and his whole appearance was that of a gallant and manly youth, whom a lady might love, or a foe might fear. Edward had not been so slow as his mistress in discovering the student's affection; and he could not but acknowledge in his heart that he was a rival not to be despised, and might yet be a successful one, if, by his means, Ellen Langton were restored to her friends. This consideration caused him to spur forward with increased ardor; but all his speed could not divest him of the idea that Fanshawe would finally overtake him, and attain the object of their mutual pursuit. There was certainly no apparent ground for this imagination: for every step of his horse increased the advantage which Edward had gained, and he soon lost sight of his rival.

Shortly after overtaking Fanshawe, the young man passed the lonely cottage formerly the residence of the Widow Butler, who now lay dead within. He was at first inclined to alight, and make inquiries respecting the fugitives; for he observed through the windows the faces of several persons, whom curiosity, or some better feeling, had led to the house of mourning.

Recollecting, however, that this portion of the road must have been passed by the angler and Ellen at too early an hour to attract notice, he forbore to waste time by a fruitless delay.

Edward proceeded on his journey, meeting with no other noticeable event, till, arriving at the summit of a hill, he beheld, a few hundred yards before him, the Rev. Dr. Melmoth. The worthy president was toiling onward at a rate unexampled in the history either of himself or his steed; the excellence of the latter consisting in sure-footedness rather than rapidity. The rider looked round, seemingly in some apprehension at the sound of hoof-tramps behind him, but was unable to conceal his satisfaction on recognizing Edward Walcott.

In the whole course of his life, Dr. Melmoth had never been placed in circumstances so embarrassing as the present. He was altogether a child in the ways of the world, having spent his youth and early manhood in abstracted study, and his maturity in the solitude of these hills. The expedition, therefore, on which fate had now thrust him, was an entire deviation from the quiet pathway of all his former years; and he felt like one who sets forth over the broad ocean without chart or compass. The affair would undoubtedly have been perplexing to a man of far more experience than he; but the doctor pictured to himself a thousand difficulties and dangers, which, except in his imagination, had no existence. The perturbation of his spirit had compelled him, more than once since his departure, to regret that he had not invited Mrs. Melmoth to a share in the adventure; this being an occasion where her firmness, decision, and confident sagacity—which made her a sort of domestic hedgehog—would have been peculiarly appropriate. In the absence of such a counsellor, even Edward Walcott—young as he was, and indiscreet as the doctor thought him—was a substitute not to be despised; and it was singular and rather ludicrous to observe how the gray-haired man unconsciously became as a child to the beardless youth. He addressed Edward with an assumption of dignity, through which his pleasure at the meeting was very obvious.

"Young gentleman, this is not well," he said. "By what authority have you absented yourself from the walls of Alma Mater during term-time?"

"I conceived that it was unnecessary to ask leave at such a conjuncture, and when the head of the institution was himself in the saddle," replied Edward.

"It was a fault, it was a fault," said Dr. Melmoth, shaking his head; "but, in consideration of the motive, I may pass it over. And now, my dear Edward, I advise that we continue our journey together, as your youth and inexperience will stand in need of the wisdom of my gray head. Nay, I pray you lay not the lash to your steed. You have ridden fast and far; and a slower pace is requisite for a season."

And, in order to keep up with his young companion, the doctor smote his own gray nag; which unhappy beast, wondering what strange concatenation of events had procured him such treatment, endeavored to obey his master's wishes. Edward had sufficient compassion for Dr. Melmoth (especially as his own horse now exhibited signs of weariness) to moderate his pace to one attainable by the former.

"Alas, youth! these are strange times," observed the president, "when a doctor of divinity and an under-graduate set forth, like a knight-errant and his squire, in search of a stray damsel. Methinks I am an epitome of the church militant, or a new species of polemical divinity. Pray Heaven, however, there be no encounter in store for us; for I utterly forgot to provide myself with weapons."

"I took some thought for that matter, reverend knight," replied Edward, whose imagination was highly tickled by Dr. Melmoth's chivalrous comparison.

"Ay, I see that you have girded on a sword," said the divine. "But wherewith shall I defend myself, my hand being empty, except of this golden headed staff, the gift of Mr. Langton?"

"One of these, if you will accept it," answered Edward, exhibiting a brace of pistols, "will serve to begin the conflict, before you join the battle hand to hand."

"Nay, I shall find little safety in meddling with that deadly instrument, since I know not accurately from which end proceeds the bullet," said Dr. Melmoth. "But were it not better, seeing we are so well provided with artillery, to betake ourselves, in the event of an encounter, to some stone-wall or other place of strength?"

"If I may presume to advise," said the squire, "you, as being most valiant and experienced, should ride forward, lance in hand (your long staff serving for a lance), while I annoy the enemy from afar."

"Like Teucer behind the shield of Ajax," interrupted Dr. Melmoth, "or David with his stone and sling. No, no, young man! I have left unfinished in my study a learned treatise, important not only to the present age, but to posterity, for whose sakes I must take heed to my safety.—But, lo! who ride yonder?" he exclaimed, in manifest alarm, pointing to some horsemen upon the brow of a hill at a short distance before them.

"Fear not, gallant leader," said Edward Walcott, who had already discovered the objects of the doctor's terror. "They are men of peace, as we shall shortly see. The foremost is somewhere near your own years, and rides like a grave, substantial citizen,—though what he does here, I know not. Behind come two servants, men likewise of sober age and pacific appearance."

"Truly your eyes are better than mine own. Of a verity, you are in the right," acquiesced Dr. Melmoth, recovering his usual quantum of intrepidity. "We will ride forward courageously, as those who, in a just cause, fear neither death nor bonds."

The reverend knight-errant and his squire, at the time of discovering the three horsemen, were within a very short distance of the town, which was, however, concealed from their view by the hill that the strangers were descending. The road from Harley College, through almost its whole extent, had been rough and wild, and the country thin of population; but now, standing frequent, amid fertile fields on each side of the way, were neat little cottages, from which groups of white-headed children rushed forth to gaze upon the travellers. The three strangers, as well as the doctor and Edward, were surrounded, as they approached each other, by a crowd of this kind, plying their little bare legs most pertinaciously in order to keep pace with the horses.

As Edward gained a nearer view of the foremost rider, his grave aspect and stately demeanor struck him with involuntary respect. There were deep lines of thought across his brow; and his calm yet bright gray eye betokened a steadfast soul. There was also an air of conscious importance, even in the manner in which the stranger sat his horse, which a man's good opinion of himself, unassisted by the concurrence of the world in general, seldom bestows. The two servants rode at a respectable distance in the rear; and the heavy portmanteaus at their backs intimated that the party had journeyed from afar. Dr. Melmoth endeavored to assume the dignity that became him as the head of Harley College; and with a gentle stroke of his staff upon his wearied steed and a grave nod to the principal stranger, was about to commence the ascent of the hill at the foot of which they were. The gentleman, however, made a halt.

"Dr. Melmoth, am I so fortunate as to meet you?" he exclaimed in accents expressive of as much surprise and pleasure as were consistent with his staid demeanor. "Have you, then, forgotten your old friend?"

"Mr. Langton! Can it be?" said the doctor, after looking him in the face a moment. "Yes, it is my old friend indeed: welcome, welcome! though you come at an unfortunate time."

"What say you? How is my child? Ellen, I trust, is well?" cried Mr. Langton, a father's anxiety overcoming the coldness and reserve that were natural to him, or that long habit had made a second nature.

"She is well in health. She was so, at least, last night," replied Dr. Melmoth unable to meet the eye of his friend. "But—but I have been a careless shepherd; and the lamb has strayed from the fold while I slept."

Edward Walcott, who was a deeply interested observer of this scene, had anticipated that a burst of passionate grief would follow the disclosure. He was, however, altogether mistaken. There was a momentary convulsion of Mr. Langton's strong features, as quick to come and go as a flash of lightning; and then his countenance was as composed—though, perhaps, a little sterner—as before. He seemed about to inquire into the particulars of what so nearly concerned him, but changed his purpose on observing the crowd of children, who, with one or two of their parents, were endeavoring to catch the words, that passed between the doctor and himself.

"I will turn back with you to the village," he said in a steady voice; "and at your leisure I shall desire to hear the particulars of this unfortunate affair."

He wheeled his horse accordingly, and, side by side with Dr. Melmoth, began to ascend the hill. On reaching the summit, the little country town lay before them, presenting a cheerful and busy spectacle. It consisted of one long, regular street, extending parallel to, and at a short distance from, the river; which here, enlarged by a junction with another stream, became navigable, not indeed for vessels of burden, but for rafts of lumber and boats of considerable size. The houses, with peaked roofs and jutting stories, stood at wide intervals along the street; and the commercial character of the place was manifested by the shop door and windows that occupied the front of almost every dwelling. One or two mansions, however, surrounded by trees, and standing back at a haughty distance from the road, were evidently the abodes of the aristocracy of the village. It was not difficult to distinguish the owners of these—self-important personages, with canes and well-powdered periwigs—among the crowd of meaner men who bestowed their attention upon Dr. Melmoth and his friend as they rode by. The town being the nearest mart of a large extent of back country, there are many rough farmers and woodsmen, to whom the cavalcade was an object of curiosity and admiration. The former feeling, indeed, was general throughout the village. The shop-keepers left their customers, and looked forth from the doors; the female portion of the community thrust their heads from the windows; and the people in the street formed a lane through which, with all eyes concentrated upon them, the party rode onward to the tavern. The general aptitude that pervades the populace of a small country town to meddle with affairs not legitimately concerning them was increased, on this occasion, by the sudden return of Mr. Langton after passing through the village. Many conjectures were afloat respecting the cause of this retrograde movement; and, by degrees, something like the truth, though much distorted, spread generally among the crowd, communicated, probably, from Mr. Langton's servants. Edward Walcott, incensed at the uncourteous curiosity of which he, as well as his companions, was the object, felt a frequent impulse (though, fortunately for himself, resisted) to make use of his riding-switch in clearing a passage.

On arriving at the tavern, Dr. Melmoth recounted to his friend the little he knew beyond the bare fact of Ellen's disappearance. Had Edward Walcott been called to their conference, he might, by disclosing the adventure of the angler, have thrown a portion of light upon the affair; but, since his first introduction, the cold and stately merchant had honored him with no sort of notice.

Edward, on his part, was not well pleased at the sudden appearance of Ellen's father, and was little inclined to cooperate in any measures that he might adopt for her recovery. It was his wish to pursue the chase on his own responsibility, and as his own wisdom dictated: he chose to be an independent ally, rather than a subordinate assistant. But, as a step preliminary to his proceedings of every other kind, he found it absolutely necessary, having journeyed far, and fasting, to call upon the landlord for a supply of food. The viands that were set before him were homely but abundant; nor were Edward's griefs and perplexities so absorbing as to overcome the appetite of youth and health.

Dr. Melmoth and Mr. Langton, after a short private conversation, had summoned the landlord, in the hope of obtaining some clew to the development of the mystery. But no young lady, nor any stranger answering to the description the doctor had received from Hugh Crombie (which was indeed a false one), had been seen to pass through the village since daybreak. Here, therefore, the friends were entirely at a loss in what direction to continue the pursuit. The village was the focus of several roads, diverging to widely distant portions of the country; and which of these the fugitives had taken, it was impossible to determine. One point, however, might be considered certain,—that the village was the first stage of their flight; for it commanded the only outlet from the valley, except a rugged path among the hills, utterly impassable by horse. In this dilemma, expresses were sent by each of the different roads; and poor Ellen's imprudence—the tale nowise decreasing as it rolled along—became known to a wide extent of country. Having thus done everything in his power to recover his daughter, the merchant exhibited a composure which Dr. Melmoth admired, but could not equal. His own mind, however, was in a far more comfortable state than when the responsibility of the pursuit had rested upon himself.

Edward Walcott, in the mean time, had employed but a very few moments in satisfying his hunger; after which his active intellect alternately formed and relinquished a thousand plans for the recovery of Ellen. Fanshawe's observation, that her flight must have commenced after the subsiding of the storm, recurred to him. On inquiry, he was informed that the violence of the rain had continued, with a few momentary intermissions, till near daylight. The fugitives must, therefore, have passed through the village long after its inhabitants were abroad; and how, without the gift of invisibility, they had contrived to elude notice, Edward could not conceive.

"Fifty years ago," thought Edward, "my sweet Ellen would have been deemed a witch for this trackless journey. Truly, I could wish I were a wizard, that I might bestride a broomstick, and follow her."

While the young man, involved in these perplexing thoughts, looked forth from the open window of the apartment, his attention was drawn to an individual, evidently of a different, though not of a higher, class than the countrymen among whom he stood. Edward now recollected that he had noticed his rough dark face among the most earnest of those who had watched the arrival of the party. He had then taken him for one of the boatmen, of whom there were many in the village, and who had much of a sailor-like dress and appearance. A second and more attentive observation, however, convinced Edward that this man's life had not been spent upon fresh water; and, had any stronger evidence than the nameless marks which the ocean impresses upon its sons been necessary, it would have been found in his mode of locomotion. While Edward was observing him, he beat slowly up to one of Mr. Langton's servants who was standing near the door of the inn. He seemed to question the man with affected carelessness; but his countenance was dark and perplexed when he turned to mingle again with the crowd. Edward lost no time in ascertaining from the servant the nature of his inquiries. They had related to the elopement of Mr. Langton's daughter, which was, indeed, the prevailing, if not the sole, subject of conversation in the village.

The grounds for supposing that this man was in any way connected with the angler were, perhaps, very slight; yet, in the perplexity of the whole affair, they induced Edward to resolve to get at the heart of his mystery. To attain this end, he took the most direct method,—by applying to the man himself.

He had now retired apart from the throng and bustle of the village, and was seated upon a condemned boat, that was drawn up to rot upon the banks of the river. His arms were folded, and his hat drawn over his brows. The lower part of his face, which alone was visible, evinced gloom and depression, as did also the deep sighs, which, because he thought no one was near him, he did not attempt to restrain.

"Friend, I must speak with you," said Edward Walcott, laying his hand upon his shoulder, after contemplating the man a moment, himself unseen.

He started at once from his abstraction and his seat, apparently expecting violence, and prepared to resist it; but, perceiving the youthful and solitary intruder upon his privacy, he composed his features with much quickness.

"What would you with me?" he asked.

"They tarry long,—or you have kept a careless watch," said Edward, speaking at a venture.

For a moment, there seemed a probability of obtaining such a reply to this observation as the youth had intended to elicit. If any trust could be put in the language of the stranger's countenance, a set of words different from those to which he subsequently gave utterance had risen to his lips. But he seemed naturally slow of speech; and this defect was now, as is frequently the case, advantageous in giving him space for reflection.

"Look you, youngster: crack no jokes on me," he at length said, contemptuously. "Away! back whence you came, or"—And he slightly waved a small rattan that he held in his right hand.

Edward's eyes sparkled, and his color rose. "You must change this tone, fellow, and that speedily," he observed. "I order you to lower your hand, and answer the questions that I shall put to you."

The man gazed dubiously at him, but finally adopted a more conciliatory mode of speech.

"Well, master; and what is your business with me?" he inquired. "I am a boatman out of employ. Any commands in my line?"

"Pshaw! I know you, my good friend, and you cannot deceive me," replied Edward Walcott. "We are private here," he continued, looking around. "I have no desire or intention to do you harm; and, if you act according to my directions, you shall have no cause to repent it."

"And what if I refuse to put myself under your orders?" inquired the man. "You are but a young captain for such an old hulk as mine."

"The ill consequences of a refusal would all be on your own side," replied Edward. "I shall, in that case, deliver you up to justice: if I have not the means of capturing you myself," he continued, observing the seaman's eye to wander rather scornfully over his youthful and slender figure, "there are hundreds within call whom it will be in vain to resist. Besides, it requires little strength to use this," he added, laying his hand on a pistol.

"If that were all, I could suit you there, my lad," muttered the stranger. He continued aloud, "Well, what is your will with me? D—d ungenteel treatment this! But put your questions; and, to oblige you, I may answer them,—if so be that I know anything of the matter."

"You will do wisely," observed the young man. "And now to business. What reason have you to suppose that the persons for whom you watch are not already beyond the village?" The seaman paused long before he answered, and gazed earnestly at Edward, apparently endeavoring to ascertain from his countenance the amount of his knowledge. This he probably overrated, but, nevertheless, hazarded a falsehood.

"I doubt not they passed before midnight," he said. "I warrant you they are many a league towards the sea-coast, ere this."

"You have kept watch, then, since midnight?" asked Edward.

"Ay, that have I! And a dark and rough one it was," answered the stranger.

"And you are certain that, if they passed at all, it must have been before that hour?"

"I kept my walk across the road till the village was all astir," said the seaman. "They could not have missed me. So, you see, your best way is to give chase; for they have a long start of you, and you have no time to lose."

"Your information is sufficient, my good friend," said Edward, with a smile. "I have reason to know that they did not commence their flight before midnight. You have made it evident that they have not passed since: ergo, they have not passed at all,—an indisputable syllogism. And now will I retrace my footsteps."

"Stay, young man," said the stranger, placing himself full in Edward's way as he was about to hasten to the inn. "You have drawn me in to betray my comrade; but, before you leave this place, you must answer a question or two of mine. Do you mean to take the law with you? or will you right your wrongs, if you have any, with your own right hand?"

"It is my intention to take the latter method. But, if I choose the former, what then?" demanded Edward. "Nay, nothing: only you or I might not have gone hence alive," replied the stranger. "But as you say he shall have fair play"—

"On my word, friend," interrupted the young man, "I fear your intelligence has come too late to do either good or harm. Look towards the inn: my companions are getting to horse, and, my life on it, they know whither to ride."

So saying, he hastened away, followed by the stranger. It was indeed evident that news of some kind or other had reached the village. The people were gathered in groups, conversing eagerly; and the pale cheeks, uplifted eyebrows, and outspread hands of some of the female sex filled Edward's mind with undefined but intolerable apprehensions. He forced his way to Dr. Melmoth, who had just mounted, and, seizing his bridle, peremptorily demanded if he knew aught of Ellen Langton.

CHAPTER VIII

"Full many a miserable year hath passed:
She knows him as one dead, or worse than dead:
And many a change her varied life hath known;
But her heart none."

MATURIN.

SINCE her interview with the angler, which was interrupted by the appearance of Fanshawe, Ellen Langton's hitherto calm and peaceful mind had been in a state of insufferable doubt and dismay. She was imperatively called upon—at least, she so conceived—to break through the rules which nature and education impose upon her sex, to quit the protection of those whose desire for her welfare was true and strong, and to trust herself, for what purpose she scarcely knew, to a stranger, from whom the instinctive purity of her mind would involuntarily have shrunk, under whatever circumstances she had met him. The letter which she had received from the hands of the angler had seemed to her inexperience to prove beyond a doubt that the bearer was the friend of her father, and authorized by him, if her duty and affection were stronger than her fears, to guide her to his retreat. The letter spoke vaguely of losses and misfortunes, and of a necessity for concealment on her father's part, and secrecy on hers; and, to the credit of Ellen's not very romantic understanding, it must be acknowledged that the mystery of the plot had nearly prevented its success. She did not, indeed, doubt that the letter was from her father's hand; for every line and stroke, and even many of its phrases, were familiar to her. Her apprehension was, that his misfortunes, of what nature soever they were, had affected his intellect, and that, under such an influence, he had commanded her to take a step which nothing less than such a command could justify. Ellen did not, however, remain long in this opinion; for when she reperused the letter, and considered the firm, regular characters, and the style,—calm and cold, even in requesting such a sacrifice,—she felt that there was nothing like insanity here. In fine, she came gradually to the belief that there were strong reasons, though incomprehensible by her, for the secrecy that her father had enjoined.

Having arrived at this conviction, her decision lay plain before her. Her affection for Mr. Langton was not, indeed,—nor was it possible,—so strong as that she would have felt for a parent who had watched over her from her infancy. Neither was the conception she had unavoidably formed of his character such as to promise that in him she would find an equivalent for all she must sacrifice. On the contrary, her gentle nature and loving heart, which otherwise would have rejoiced in a new object of affection, now shrank with something like dread from the idea of meeting her father,—stately, cold, and stern as she could not but imagine him. A sense of duty was therefore Ellen's only support in resolving to tread the dark path that lay before her.

Had there been any person of her own sex in whom Ellen felt confidence, there is little doubt that she would so far have disobeyed her father's letter as to communicate its contents, and take counsel as to her proceedings. But Mrs. Melmoth was the only female—excepting, indeed, the maid-servant—to whom it was possible to make the communication; and, though Ellen at first thought of such a step, her timidity, and her knowledge of the lady's character, did not permit her to venture upon it. She next reviewed her acquaintances of the other sex; and Dr. Melmoth first presented himself, as in every respect but one, an unexceptionable confidant. But the single exception was equivalent to many. The maiden, with the highest opinion of the doctor's learning and talents, had sufficient penetration to know, that, in the ways of the world, she was herself the better skilled of the two. For a moment she thought of Edward Walcott; but he was light and wild, and, which her

delicacy made an insurmountable objection, there was an un-
told love between them. Her thoughts finally centred on Fanshawe. In his judgment, young and inexperienced though he
was, she would have placed a firm trust; and his zeal, from
whatever cause it arose, she could not doubt.

If, in the short time allowed her for reflection, an opportunity had occurred for consulting him, she would, in all probability, have taken advantage of it. But the terms on which they
had parted the preceding evening had afforded him no reason
to hope for her confidence; and he felt that there were others
who had a better right to it than himself. He did not, therefore,
throw himself in her way; and poor Ellen was consequently
left without an adviser.

The determination that resulted from her own unassisted
wisdom has been seen. When discovered by Dr. Melmoth at
Hugh Crombie's inn, she was wholly prepared for flight, and,
but for the intervention of the storm, would, ere then, have
been far away.

The firmness of resolve that had impelled a timid maiden
upon such a step was not likely to be broken by one defeat; and
Ellen, accordingly, confident that the stranger would make a
second attempt, determined that no effort on her part should
be wanting to its success. On reaching her chamber, therefore, instead of retiring to rest (of which, from her sleepless
thoughts of the preceding night, she stood greatly in need),
she sat watching for the abatement of the storm. Her medita-
tions were now calmer than at any time since her first meeting with the angler. She felt as if her fate was decided. The
stain had fallen upon her reputation: she was no longer the
same pure being in the opinion of those whose approbation
she most valued.

One obstacle to her flight—and, to a woman's mind, a most
powerful one—had thus been removed. Dark and intricate as
was the way, it was easier now to proceed than to pause; and
her desperate and forlorn situation gave her a strength which
hitherto she had not felt.

At every cessation in the torrent of rain that beat against
the house, Ellen flew to the window, expecting to see the
stranger form beneath it. But the clouds would again thicken,

and the storm recommence with its former violence; and she began to fear that the approach of morning would compel her to meet the now dreaded face of Dr. Melmoth. At length, however, a strong and steady wind, supplying the place of the fitful gusts of the preceding part of the night, broke and scattered the clouds from the broad expanse of the sky. The moon, commencing her late voyage not long before the sun, was now visible, setting forth like a lonely ship from the dark line of the horizon, and touching at many a little silver cloud the islands of that aerial deep. Ellen felt that now the time was come; and, with a calmness wonderful to herself, she prepared for her final departure.

She had not long to wait ere she saw, between the vacancies of the trees, the angler advancing along the shady avenue that led to the principal entrance of Dr. Melmoth's dwelling. He had no need to summon her either by word or signal; for she had descended, emerged from the door, and stood before him, while he was yet at some distance from the house.

"You have watched well," he observed in a low, strange tone. "As saith the Scripture, 'Many daughters have done virtuously; but thou excellest them all.'"

He took her arm; and they hastened down the avenue. Then, leaving Hugh Crombie's inn on their right, they found its master in a spot so shaded that the moonbeams could not enlighten it. He held by the bridle two horses, one of which the angler assisted Ellen to mount. Then, turning to the landlord he pressed a purse into his hand; but Hugh drew back, and it fell to the ground.

"No! this would not have tempted me; nor will it reward me," he said. "If you have gold to spare, there are some that need it more than I."

"I understand you, mine host. I shall take thought for them; and enough will remain for you and me," replied his comrade. "I have seen the day when such a purse would not have slipped between your fingers. Well, be it so. And now, Hugh, my old friend, a shake of your hand; for we are seeing our last of each other."

"Pray Heaven it be so! though I wish you no ill," said the landlord, giving his hand.

He then seemed about to approach Ellen, who had been unable to distinguish the words of this brief conversation; but his comrade prevented him. "There is no time to lose," he observed. "The moon is growing pale already, and we should have been many a mile beyond the valley ere this." He mounted as he spoke; and, guiding Ellen's rein till they reached the road, they dashed away.

It was now that she felt herself completely in his power; and with that consciousness there came a sudden change of feeling, and an altered view of her conduct. A thousand reasons forced themselves upon her mind, seeming to prove that she had been deceived; while the motives, so powerful with her but a moment before, had either vanished from her memory or lost all their efficacy. Her companion, who gazed searchingly into her face, where the moonlight, coming down between the pines, allowed him to read its expression, probably discerned somewhat of the state of her thoughts.

"Do you repent so soon?" he inquired. "We have a weary way before us. Faint not ere we have well entered upon it."

"I have left dear friends behind me, and am going I know not whither," replied Ellen, tremblingly.

"You have a faithful guide," he observed, turning away his head, and speaking in the tone of one who endeavors to smother a laugh.

Ellen had no heart to continue the conversation; and they rode on in silence, and through a wild and gloomy scene. The wind roared heavily through the forest, and the trees shed their raindrops upon the travellers. The road, at all times rough, was now broken into deep gullies, through which streams went murmuring down to mingle with the river. The pale moonlight combined with the gray of the morning to give a ghastly and unsubstantial appearance to every object.

The difficulties of the road had been so much increased by the storm, that the purple eastern clouds gave notice of the near approach of the sun just as the travellers reached the little lonesome cottage which Ellen remembered to have visited several months before. On arriving opposite to it, her companion checked his horse, and gazed with a wild earnestness at the wretched habitation. Then, stifling a groan that would not altogether be repressed, he was about to pass on; but at that moment the cottage-door opened, and a woman, whose sour, unpleasant countenance Ellen recognized, came hastily forth. She seemed not to heed the travellers; but the angler, his voice thrilling and quivering with indescribable emotion, addressed her.

"Woman, whither do you go?" he inquired.

She started, but, after a momentary pause, replied, "There is one within at the point of death. She struggles fearfully; and I cannot endure to watch alone by her bedside. If you are Christians, come in with me."

Ellen's companion leaped hastily from his horse, assisted her also to dismount, and followed the woman into the cottage, having first thrown the bridles of the horses carelessly over the branch of a tree. Ellen trembled at the awful scene she would be compelled to witness; but, when death was so near at hand, it was more terrible to stand alone in the dim morning light than even to watch the parting of soul and body. She therefore entered the cottage.

Her guide, his face muffled in his cloak, had taken his stand at a Distance from the death-bed, in a part of the room which neither the increasing daylight nor the dim rays of a solitary lamp had yet enlightened. At Ellen's entrance, the dying woman lay still, and apparently calm, except that a plaintive, half-articulate sound occasionally wandered through her lips.

"Hush! For mercy's sake, silence!" whispered the other woman to the strangers. "There is good hope now that she will die a peaceable death; but, if she is disturbed, the boldest of us will not dare to stand by her bedside."

The whisper by which her sister endeavored to preserve quiet perhaps reached the ears of the dying female; for she now raised herself in bed, slowly, but with a strength superior to what her situation promised. Her face was ghastly and wild, from long illness, approaching death, and disturbed intellect; and a disembodied spirit could scarcely be a more fearful object than one whose soul was just struggling forth. Her sister, approaching with the soft and stealing step appropriate to the chamber of sickness and death, attempted to replace the covering around her, and to compose her again upon the pillow. "Lie down and sleep, sister," she said; "and, when the day breaks, I will waken you. Methinks your breath comes freer already. A little more slumber, and to-morrow you will be well."

"My illness is gone: I am well," said the dying-woman, gasping for breath. "I wander where the fresh breeze comes sweetly over my face; but a close and stifled air has choked my lungs."

"Yet a little while, and you will no longer draw your breath in pain," observed her sister, again replacing the bedclothes, which she continued to throw off.

"My husband is with me," murmured the widow. "He walks by my side, and speaks to me as in old times; but his words come faintly on my ear. Cheer me and comfort me, my husband; for there is a terror in those dim, motionless eyes, and in that shadowy voice."

As she spoke thus, she seemed to gaze upon some object that stood by her bedside; and the eyes of those who witnessed this scene could not but follow the direction of hers. They observed that the dying woman's own shadow was marked upon the wall, receiving a tremulous motion from the fitful rays of the lamp, and from her own convulsive efforts. "My husband stands gazing on me," she said again; "but my son,—where is he? And, as I ask, the father turns away his face. Where is our son? For his sake, I have longed to come to this land of rest. For him I have sorrowed many years. Will he not comfort me now?"

At these words the stranger made a few hasty steps towards the bed; but, ere he reached it, he conquered the impulse that drew him thither, and, shrouding his face more deeply in his cloak, returned to his former position. The dying woman, in the mean time, had thrown herself back upon the bed; and her sobbing and wailing, imaginary as was their cause, were inexpressibly affecting.

"Take me back to earth," she said; "for its griefs have followed me hither."

The stranger advanced, and, seizing the lamp, knelt down by the bedside, throwing the light full upon his pale and convulsed features.

"Mother, here is your son!" he exclaimed.

At that unforgotten voice, the darkness burst away at once from her soul. She arose in bed, her eyes and her whole countenance beaming with joy, and threw her arms about his neck. A multitude of words seemed struggling for utterance; but they gave place to a low moaning sound, and then to the silence of death. The one moment of happiness, that recompensed years of sorrow, had been her last. Her son laid the lifeless form upon the pillow, and gazed with fixed eyes on his mother's face.

As he looked, the expression of enthusiastic joy that parting life had left upon the features faded gradually away; and the countenance, though no longer wild, assumed the sadness which it had worn through a long course of grief and pain. On beholding this natural consequence of death, the thought, perhaps, occurred to him, that her soul, no longer dependent on the imperfect means of intercourse possessed by mortals, had communed with his own, and become acquainted with all its guilt and misery. He started from the bedside, and covered his face with his hands, as if to hide it from those dead eyes.

Such a scene as has been described could not but have a powerful effect upon any one who retained aught of humanity; and the grief of the son, whose natural feelings had been blunted, but not destroyed, by an evil life, was much more violent than his outward demeanor would have expressed. But his deep repentance for the misery he had brought upon his parent did not produce in him a resolution to do wrong no more. The sudden consciousness of accumulated guilt made him desperate. He felt as if no one had thenceforth a claim to justice or compassion at his hands, when his neglect and cruelty had poisoned his mother's life, and hastened her death.

Thus it was that the Devil wrought with him to his own destruction, reversing the salutary effect which his mother would have died exultingly to produce upon his mind. He now turned to Ellen Langton with a demeanor singularly calm and composed.

"We must resume our journey," he said, in his usual tone of voice. "The sun is on the point of rising, though but little light finds its way into this hovel."

Ellen's previous suspicions as to the character of her companion had now become certainty so far as to convince her that she was in the power of a lawless and guilty man; though what fate he intended for her she was unable to conjecture. An open opposition to his will, however, could not be ventured upon; especially as she discovered, on looking round the apartment, that, with the exception of the corpse, they were alone.

"Will you not attend your mother's funeral?" she asked, trembling, and conscious that he would discover her fears.

"The dead must bury their dead," he replied. "I have brought my mother to her grave,—and what can a son do more? This purse, however, will serve to lay her in the earth, and leave something for the old hag. Whither is she gone?" interrupted he, casting a glance round the room in search of the old woman. "Nay, then, we must speedily to horse. I know her of old."

Thus saying, he threw the purse upon the table, and, without trusting himself to look again towards the dead, conducted Ellen out of the cottage. The first rays of the sun at that moment gilded the tallest trees of the forest.

On looking towards the spot were the horses had stood, Ellen thought that Providence, in answer to her prayers, had taken care for her deliverance. They were no longer there,—a circumstance easily accounted for by the haste with which the bridles had been thrown over the branch of the tree. Her companion, however, imputed it to another cause.

"The hag! She would sell her own flesh and blood by weight and measure," he muttered to himself. "This is some plot of hers, I know well."

He put his hand to his forehead for a moment's space, seeming to reflect on the course most advisable to be pursued. Ellen, perhaps unwisely, interposed.

"Would it not be well to return?" she asked, timidly. "There is now no hope of escaping; but I might yet reach home undiscovered."

"Return!" repeated her guide, with a look and smile from which she turned away her face. "Have you forgotten your father and his misfortunes? No, no, sweet Ellen: it is too late for such thoughts as these."

He took her hand, and led her towards the forest, in the rear of the cottage. She would fain have resisted; but they were all alone, and the attempt must have been both fruit-less and dangerous. She therefore trod with him a path so devious, so faintly traced, and so overgrown with bushes and young trees, that only a most accurate acquaintance in his early days could have enabled her guide to retain it. To him, however, it seemed so perfectly familiar, that he was not once compelled to pause, though the numerous windings soon deprived Ellen of all knowledge of the situation of the cottage. They descended a steep hill, and, proceeding par-allel to the river,—as Ellen judged by its rushing sound,—at length found themselves at what proved to be the termina-tion of their walk.

Ellen now recollected a remark of Edward Walcott's re-specting the wild and rude scenery through which the river here kept its way; and, in less agitating circumstances, her pleasure and admiration would have been great. They stood beneath a precipice, so high that the loftiest pine-tops (and many of them seemed to soar to heaven) scarcely surmounted it. This line of rock has a considerable extent, at unequal heights, and with many interruptions, along the course of the river; and it seems probable that, at some former period, it was the boundary of the waters, though they are now confined within far less ambitious limits. The inferior portion of the crag, beneath which Ellen and her guide were standing, varies so far from the perpendic-ular as not to be inaccessible by a careful footstep. But only one person has been known to attempt the ascent of the superior half, and only one the descent; yet, steep as is the height, trees and bushes of various kinds have clung to the rock, wherever their roots could gain the slightest hold; thus seeming to prefer the scanty and difficult nourishment of the cliff to a more luxu-rious life in the rich interval that extends from its base to the river. But, whether or no these hardy vegetables have voluntari-ly chosen their rude resting-place, the cliff is indebted to them for much of the beauty that tempers its sublimity. When the eye is pained and wearied by the bold nakedness of the rock, it rests with pleasure on the cheerful foliage of the birch, or upon the darker green of the funereal pine. Just at the termination of the accessible portion of the crag, these trees are so numerous, and their foliage so dense, that they completely shroud from view a considerable excavation, formed, probably, hundreds of years since, by the fall of a portion of the rock. The detached fragment still lies at a little distance from the base, gray and moss-grown, but corresponding, in its general outline, to the cavity from which it was rent.

But the most singular and beautiful object in all this scene is a tiny fount of crystal water, that gushes forth from the high, smooth forehead of the cliff. Its perpendicular descent is of many feet; after which it finds its way, with a sweet diminutive murmur, to the level ground.

It is not easy to conceive whence the barren rock procures even the small supply of water that is necessary to the existence of this stream; it is as unaccountable as the gush of gentle feeling which sometimes proceeds from the hardest heart: but there it continues to flow and fall, undiminished and unincreased. The stream is so slender, that the gentlest breeze suffices to disturb its descent, and to scatter its pure sweet waters over the face of the cliff. But in that deep forest there is seldom a breath of wind; so that, plashing continually upon one spot, the fount has worn its own little channel of white sand, by which it finds its way to the river. Alas that the Naiades have lost their old authority! for what a deity of tiny loveliness must once have presided here!

Ellen's companion paused not to gaze either upon the loveliness or the sublimity of this scene, but, assisting her where it was requisite, began the steep and difficult ascent of the lower part of the cliff. The maiden's ingenuity in vain endeavored to assign reasons for this movement; but when they reached the tuft of trees, which, as has been noticed, grew at the ultimate point where mortal footstep might safely tread, she perceived through their thick branches the recess in the rock. Here they entered; and her guide pointed to a mossy seat, in the formation of which, to judge from its regularity, art had probably a share.

"Here you may remain in safety," he observed, "till I obtain the means of proceeding. In this spot you need fear no intruder; but it will be dangerous to venture beyond its bounds."

The meaning glance that accompanied these words intimated to poor Ellen, that, in warning her against danger, he alluded to the vengeance with which he would visit any attempt to escape. To leave her thus alone, trusting to the influence of such a threat, was a bold, yet a necessary and by no means a hopeless measure. On Ellen it produced the desired effect; and she sat in the cave as motionless, for a time, as if she had herself been a part of the rock. In other circumstances this shady recess would have been a delightful retreat during the sultry warmth of a summer's day. The dewy coolness of the rock kept the air always fresh and the sunbeams never thrust themselves so as to dissipate the mellow twilight through the green trees with which the chamber was curtained. Ellen's sleeplessness and agitation for many preceding hours had perhaps deadened her feelings; for she now felt a sort of indifference creeping upon her, an inability to realize the evils of her situation, at the same time that she was perfectly aware of them all. This torpor of mind increased, till her eyelids began to grow heavy and the cave and trees to swim before her sight. In a few moments more she would probably have been in dreamless slumber; but, rousing herself by a strong effort, she looked round the narrow limits of the cave in search of objects to excite her worn-out mind.

She now perceived, wherever the smooth rock afforded place for them, the initials, or the full-length names of former visitants of the cave. What wanderer on mountain-tops or in deep solitudes has not felt the influence of these records of humanity, telling him, when such a conviction is soothing to his heart, that he is not alone in the world? It was singular, that, when her own mysterious situation had almost lost its power to engage her thoughts, Ellen perused these barren memorials with a certain degree of interest. She went on repeating them aloud, and starting at the sound of her own voice, till at length, as one name passed through her lips, she paused, and then, leaning her forehead against the letters, burst into tears. It was the name of Edward Walcott; and it struck upon her heart, arousing her to a full sense of her present misfortunes and dangers, and, more painful still, of her past happiness. Her tears had, however, a soothing, and at the same time a strengthening effect upon her mind; for, when their gush was over, she raised her head, and began to meditate on the means of escape. She wondered at the species of fascination that had kept her, as if chained to the rock, so long, when there was, in reality, nothing to bar her pathway. She determined, late as it was, to attempt her own deliverance, and for that purpose began slowly and cautiously to emerge from the cave.

Peeping out from among the trees, she looked and listened with most painful anxiety to discover if any living thing were in that seeming solitude, or if any sound disturbed the heavy stillness. But she saw only Nature in her wildest forms, and heard only the plash and murmur (almost inaudible, because continual) of the little waterfall, and the quick, short throbbing of her own heart, against which she pressed her hand as if to hush it. Gathering courage, therefore, she began to descend; and, starting often at the loose stones that even her light footstep displaced and sent rattling down, she at length reached the base of the crag in safety. She then made a few steps in the direction, as nearly as she could judge, by which she arrived at the spot, but paused, with a sudden revulsion of the blood to her heart, as her guide emerged from behind a projecting part of the rock. He approached her deliberately, an ironical smile writhing his features into a most disagreeable expression; while in his eyes there was something that seemed a wild, fierce joy. By a species of sophistry, of which oppressors often make use, he had brought himself to believe that he was now the injured one, and that Ellen, by her distrust of him, had fairly subjected herself to whatever evil it consisted with his will and power to inflict upon her. Her only restraining influence over him, the consciousness, in his own mind, that he possessed her confidence, was now done away. Ellen, as well as her enemy, felt that this was the case. She knew not what to dread; but she was well aware that danger was at hand, and that, in the deep wilderness, there was none to help her, except that Being with whose inscrutable purposes it might consist to allow the wicked to triumph for a season, and the innocent to be brought low.

"Are you so soon weary of this quiet retreat?" demanded her guide, continuing to wear the same sneering smile. "Or has your anxiety for your father induced you to set forth alone in quest of the afflicted old man?"

"Oh, if I were but with him!" exclaimed Ellen. "But this place is lonely and fearful; and I cannot endure to remain here."

"Lonely, is it, sweet Ellen?" he rejoined; "am I not with you? Yes, it is lonely,—lonely as guilt could wish. Cry aloud, Ellen, and spare not. Shriek, and see if there be any among these rocks and woods to hearken to you!"

"There is, there is One," exclaimed Ellen, shuddering, and affrighted at the fearful meaning of his countenance. "He is here! He is there!" And she pointed to heaven.

"It may be so, dearest," he replied. "But if there be an Ear that hears, and an Eye that sees all the evil of the earth, yet the Arm is slow to avenge. Else why do I stand before you a living man?"

"His vengeance may be delayed for a time, but not forever," she answered, gathering a desperate courage from the extremity of her fear.

"You say true, lovely Ellen; and I have done enough, erenow, to insure its heaviest weight. There is a pass, when evil deeds can add nothing to guilt, nor good ones take anything from it."

"Think of your mother,—of her sorrow through life, and perhaps even after death," Ellen began to say. But, as she spoke these words, the expression of his face was changed, becoming suddenly so dark and fiend-like, that she clasped her hands, and fell on her knees before him.

"I have thought of my mother," he replied, speaking very low, and putting his face close to hers. "I remember the neglect, the wrong, the lingering and miserable death, that she received at my hands. By what claim can either man or woman henceforth expect mercy from me? If God will help you, be it so; but by those words you have turned my heart to stone."

At this period of their conversation, when Ellen's peril seemed most imminent, the attention of both was attracted by a fragment of rock, which, falling from the summit of the crag, struck very near them. Ellen started from her knees, and, with her false guide, gazed eagerly upward,—he in the fear of interruption, she in the hope of deliverance.

CHAPTER IX

"At length, he cries, behold the fated spring!
Yon rugged cliff conceals the fountain blest,
Dark rocks its crystal source o'ershadowing."

PSYCHE

THE tale now returns to Fanshawe, who, as will be recollected, after being overtaken by Edward Walcott, was left with little apparent prospect of aiding in the deliverance of Ellen Langton.

It would be difficult to analyze the feelings with which the student pursued the chase, or to decide whether he was influenced and animated by the same hopes of successful love that cheered his rival. That he was conscious of such hopes, there is little reason to suppose; for the most powerful minds are not always the best acquainted with their own feelings. Had Fanshawe, moreover, acknowledged to himself the possibility of gaining Ellen's affections, his generosity would have induced him to refrain from her society before it was too late. He had read her character with accuracy, and had seen how fit she was to love, and to be loved, by a man who could find his happiness in the common occupations of the world; and Fanshawe never deceived himself so far as to suppose that this would be the case with him. Indeed, he often wondered at the passion with which Ellen's simple loveliness of mind and person had inspired him, and which seemed to be founded on the principle of contrariety, rather than of sympathy. It was the yearning of a soul, formed by Nature in a peculiar mould, for communion with those to whom it bore a resemblance, yet of whom it was not. But there was no reason to suppose that Ellen, who differed from the multitude only as being purer and better, would cast away her affections on the one, of all who surrounded her, least fitted to make her happy. Thus Fanshawe reasoned with himself, and of this he believed that he was convinced. Yet ever and anon he found himself involved in a dream of bliss, of which Ellen was to be the giver and the sharer. Then would he rouse himself, and press upon his mind the chilling consciousness that it was and could be but a dream. There was also another feeling, apparently discordant with those which have been enumerated. It was a longing for rest, for his old retirement, that came at intervals so powerfully upon him, as he rode on, that his heart sickened of the active exertion on which fate had thrust him.

After being overtaken by Edward Walcott, Fanshawe continued his journey with as much speed as was attainable by his wearied horse, but at a pace infinitely too slow for his earnest thoughts. These had carried him far away, leaving him only such a consciousness of his present situation as to make diligent use of the spur, when a horse's tread at no great distance struck upon his ear. He looked forward and behind; but, though a considerable extent of the narrow, rocky, and grass-grown road was visible, he was the only traveller there. Yet again he heard the sound, which, he now discovered, proceeded from among the trees that lined the roadside. Alighting, he entered the forest, with the intention, if the steed proved to be disengaged, and superior to his own, of appropriating him to his own use. He soon gained a view of the object he sought; but the animal rendered a closer acquaintance unattainable, by immediately taking to his heels. Fanshawe had, however, made a most interesting discovery; for the horse was accoutred with a side-saddle; and who but Ellen Langton could have been his rider? At this conclusion, though his perplexity was thereby in no degree diminished, the student immediately arrived. Returning to the road, and perceiving on the summit of the hill a cottage, which he recognized as the one he had entered with Ellen and Edward Walcott, he determined there to make inquiry respecting the objects of his pursuit.

On reaching the door of the poverty-stricken dwelling, he saw that it was not now so desolate of inmates as on his previous visit. In the single inhabitable apartment were several elderly women, clad evidently in their well-worn and well-saved Sunday clothes, and all wearing a deep grievous expression of countenance. Fanshawe was not long in deciding that death was within the cottage, and that these aged females were of the class who love the house of mourning, because to them it is a house of feasting. It is a fact, disgusting and lamentable, that the disposition which Heaven, for the best of purposes, has implanted in the female breast—to watch by the sick and comfort the afflicted—frequently becomes depraved into an odious love of scenes of pain and death and sorrow. Such women are like the Ghouls of the Arabian Tales, whose feasting was among tombstones and upon dead carcasses.

(It is sometimes, though less frequently, the case, that this disposition to make a "joy of grief" extends to individuals of the other sex. But in us it is even less excusable and more disgusting, because it is our nature to shun the sick and afflicted; and, unless restrained by principles other than we bring into the world with us, men might follow the example of many animals in destroying the infirm of their own species. Indeed, instances of this nature might be adduced among savage nations.) Sometimes, however, from an original *lusus naturae,* or from the influence of circumstances, a man becomes a haunter of death-beds, a tormentor of afflicted hearts, and a follower of funerals. Such an abomination now appeared before Fanshawe, and beckoned him into the cottage. He was considerably beyond the middle age, rather corpulent, with a broad, fat, tallow-complexioned countenance. The student obeyed his silent call, and entered the room, through the open door of which he had been gazing.

He now beheld, stretched out upon the bed where she had so lately lain in life, though dying, the yet uncoffined corpse of the aged woman, whose death has been described. How frightful it seemed!—that fixed countenance of ashy paleness, amid its decorations of muslin and fine linen, as if a bride were decked for the marriage-chamber, as if death were a bridegroom, and the coffin a bridal bed. Alas that the vanity of dress should extend even to the grave!

The female who, as being the near and only relative of the deceased, was supposed to stand in need of comfort, was surrounded by five or six of her own sex. These continually poured into her ear the stale, trite maxims which, where consolation is actually required, add torture insupportable to the wounded heart. Their present object, however, conducted herself with all due decorum, holding her handkerchief to her tearless eyes, and answering with very grievous groans to the words of her comforters. Who could have imagined that there was joy in her heart, because, since her sister's death, there was but one remaining obstacle between herself and the sole property of that wretched cottage?

While Fanshawe stood silently observing this scene, a low, monotonous voice was uttering some words in his ear, of the meaning of which his mind did not immediately take note. He turned, and saw that the speaker was the person who had invited him to enter.

"What is your pleasure with me, sir?" demanded the student.

"I make bold to ask," replied the man, "whether you would choose to partake of some creature comfort, before joining in prayer with the family and friends of our deceased sister?" As he spoke, he pointed to a table, on which was a moderate-sized stone jug and two or three broken glasses; for then, as now, there were few occasions of joy or grief on which ardent spirits were not considered indispensable, to heighten the one or to alleviate the other.

"I stand in no need of refreshment," answered Fanshawe; "and it is not my intention to pray at present."

"I pray your pardon, reverend sir," rejoined the other; "but your face is pale, and you look wearied. A drop from yonder vessel is needful to recruit the outward man. And for the prayer, the sisters will expect it; and their souls are longing for the outpouring of the Spirit. I was intending to open my own mouth with such words as are given to my poor ignorance, but"—

Fanshawe was here about to interrupt this address, which proceeded on the supposition, arising from his black dress and thoughtful countenance, that he was a clergyman. But one of the females now approached him, and intimated that the sister of the deceased was desirous of the benefit of his conversation. He would have returned a negative to this request, but, looking towards the afflicted woman, he saw her withdraw her handkerchief from her eyes, and cast a brief but penetrating and most intelligent glance upon him. He immediately expressed his readiness to offer such consolation as might be in his power.

"And in the mean time," observed the lay-preacher, "I will give the sisters to expect a word of prayer and exhortation, either from you or from myself."

These words were lost upon the supposed clergyman, who was already at the side of the mourner. The females withdrew out of ear-shot to give place to a more legitimate comforter than themselves.

"What know you respecting my purpose?" inquired Fanshawe, bending towards her.

The woman gave a groan—the usual result of all efforts at consolation—for the edification of the company, and then replied in a whisper, which reached only the ear for which it was intended. "I know whom you come to seek: I can direct you to them. Speak low, for God's sake!" she continued, observing that Fanshawe was about to utter an exclamation. She then resumed her groans with greater zeal than before.

"Where—where are they?" asked the student, in a whisper which all his efforts could scarcely keep below his breath. "I adjure you to tell me."

"And, if I should, how am I like to be bettered by it?" inquired the old woman, her speech still preceded and followed by a groan.

"O God! The *auri sacra fames!*" thought Fanshawe with, a sickening heart, looking at the motionless corpse upon the bed, and then at the wretched being, whom the course of nature, in comparatively a moment of time, would reduce to the same condition.

He whispered again, however, putting his purse into the hag's hand. "Take this. Make your own terms when they are discovered. Only tell me where I must seek them—and speedily, or it may be too late."

"I am a poor woman, and am afflicted," said she, taking the purse, unseen by any who were in the room. "It is little that worldly goods can do for me, and not long can I enjoy them." And here she was delivered of a louder and a more heartfelt groan than ever. She then continued: "Follow the path behind the cottage, that leads to the river-side. Walk along the foot of the rock, and search for them near the water-spout. Keep a slow pace till you are out of sight," she added, as the student started to his feet. The guests of the cottage did not attempt to oppose Fanshawe's progress, when they saw him take the path towards the forest, imagining, probably, that he was retiring for the purpose of secret prayer. But the old woman laughed behind the handkerchief with which she veiled her face.

"Take heed to your steps, boy," she muttered; "for they are leading you whence you will not return. Death, too, for the slayer. Be it so."

Fanshawe, in the mean while, contrived to discover, and for a while to retain, the narrow and winding path that led to the river-side. But it was originally no more than a track, by which the cattle belonging to the cottage went down to their watering-place, and by these four-footed passengers it had long been deserted.

The fern-bushes, therefore, had grown over it; and in several places trees of considerable size had shot up in the midst. These difficulties could scarcely have been surmounted by the utmost caution; and as Fanshawe's thoughts were too deeply fixed upon the end to pay a due regard to the means, he soon became desperately bewildered both as to the locality of the river and of the cottage. Had he known, however, in which direction to seek the latter, he would not, probably, have turned back; not that he was infected by any chivalrous desire to finish the adventure alone, but because he would expect little assistance from those he had left there. Yet he could not but wonder—though he had not in his first eagerness taken notice of it—at the anxiety of the old woman that he should proceed singly, and without the knowledge of her guests, on the search. He nevertheless continued to wander on,—pausing often to listen for the rush of the river, and then starting forward with fresh rapidity, to rid himself of the sting of his own thoughts, which became painfully intense when undisturbed by bodily motion. His way was now frequently interrupted by rocks, that thrust their huge gray heads from the ground, compelling him to turn aside, and thus depriving him, fortunately, perhaps, of all remaining idea of the direction he had intended to pursue.

Thus he went on, his head turned back, and taking little heed to his footsteps, when, perceiving that he trod upon a smooth, level rock, he looked forward, and found himself almost on the utmost verge of a precipice.

After the throbbing of the heart that followed this narrow escape had subsided, he stood gazing down where the sunbeams slept so pleasantly at the roots of the tall old trees, with whose highest tops he was upon a level. Suddenly he seemed to hear voices—one well-remembered voice—ascending from beneath; and, approaching to the edge of the cliff, he saw at its base the two whom he sought.

He saw and interpreted Ellen's look and attitude of entreaty, though the words with which she sought to soften the ruthless heart of her guide became inaudible ere they reached the height where Fanshawe stood. He felt that Heaven had sent him thither, at the moment of her utmost need, to be the preserver of all that was dear to him; and he paused only to consider the mode in which her deliverance was to be effected. Life he would have laid down willingly, exultingly: his only care was, that the sacrifice should not be in vain.

At length, when Ellen fell upon her knees, he lifted a small fragment of rock, and threw it down the cliff. It struck so near the pair, that it immediately drew the attention of both.

When the betrayer, at the instant in which he had almost defied the power of the Omnipotent to bring help to Ellen, became aware of Fanshawe's presence, his hardihood failed him for a time, and his knees actually tottered beneath him. There was something awful, to his apprehension, in the slight form that stood so far above him, like a being from another sphere, looking down upon his wickedness. But his half-superstitious dread endured only a moment's space; and then, mustering the courage that in a thousand dangers had not deserted him, he prepared to revenge the intrusion by which Fanshawe had a second time interrupted his designs.

"By Heaven, I will cast him down at her feet!" he muttered through his closed teeth. "There shall be no form nor likeness of man left in him. Then let him rise up, if he is able, and defend her."

Thus resolving, and overlooking all hazard in his eager hatred and desire for vengeance, he began a desperate attempt to ascend the cliff. The space which only had hitherto been deemed accessible was quickly passed; and in a moment more he was half-way up the precipice, clinging to trees, shrubs, and projecting portions of the rock, and escaping through hazards which seemed to menace inevitable destruction.

Fanshawe, as he watched his upward progress, deemed that every step would be his last; but when he perceived that more than half, and apparently the most difficult part, of the ascent was surmounted, his opinion changed. His courage, however, did not fail him as the moment of need drew nigh. His spirits rose buoyantly; his limbs seemed to grow firm and strong; and he stood on the edge of the precipice, prepared for the death-struggle which would follow the success of his enemy's attempt.

But that attempt was not successful. When within a few feet of the summit, the adventurer grasped at a twig too slenderly rooted to sustain his weight. It gave way in his hand, and he fell backward down the precipice. His head struck against the less perpendicular part of the rock, whence the body rolled heavily down to the detached fragment, of which mention has heretofore been made. There was no life left in him. With all the passions of hell alive in his heart, he had met the fate that he intended for Fanshawe.

The student paused not then to shudder at the sudden and awful overthrow of his enemy; for he saw that Ellen lay motionless at the foot of the cliff. She had indeed fainted at the moment she became aware of her deliverer's presence; and no stronger proof could she have given of her firm reliance upon his protection.

Fanshawe was not deterred by the danger, of which he had just received so fearful an evidence, from attempting to descend to her assistance; and, whether owing to his advantage in lightness of frame, or to superior caution, he arrived safely at the base of the precipice.

He lifted the motionless form of Ellen in his arms, and, resting her head against his shoulder, gazed on her cheek of lily paleness with a joy, a triumph, that rose almost to madness. It contained no mixture of hope; it had no reference to the future: it was the perfect bliss of a moment,—an insulated point of happiness. He bent over her, and pressed a kiss—the first, and he knew it would be the last—on her pale lips; then, bearing her to the fountain, he sprinkled its waters profusely over her face, neck, and bosom. She at length opened her eyes, slowly and heavily; but her mind was evidently wandering, till Fanshawe spoke.

"Fear not, Ellen. You are safe," he said.

At the sound of his voice, her arm, which was thrown over his shoulder, involuntarily tightened its embrace, telling him, by that mute motion, with how firm a trust she confided in him. But, as a fuller sense of her situation returned, she raised herself to her feet, though still retaining the support of his arm. It was singular, that, although her insensibility had commenced before the fall of her guide, she turned away her eyes, as if instinctively, from the spot where the mangled body lay; nor did she inquire of Fanshawe the manner of her deliverance.

"Let us begone from this place," she said in faint, low accents, and with an inward shudder.

They walked along the precipice, seeking some passage by which they might gain its summit, and at length arrived at that by which Ellen and her guide had descended. Chance—for neither Ellen nor Fanshawe could have discovered the path—led them, after but little wandering, to the cottage. A messenger was sent forward to the town to inform Dr. Melmoth of the recovery of his ward; and the intelligence thus received had interrupted Edward Walcott's conversation with the seaman.

It would have been impossible, in the mangled remains of Ellen's guide, to discover the son of the Widow Butler, except from the evidence of her sister, who became, by his death, the sole inheritrix of the cottage. The history of this evil and unfortunate man must be comprised within very narrow limits. A harsh father, and his own untamable disposition, had driven him from home in his boyhood; and chance had made him the temporary companion of Hugh Crombie. After two years of wandering, when in a foreign country and in circumstances of utmost need, he attracted the notice of Mr. Langton. The merchant took his young countryman under his protection, afforded him advantages of education, and, as his capacity was above mediocrity, gradually trusted him in many affairs of importance. During this period, there was no evidence of dishonesty on his part. On the contrary, he manifested a zeal for Mr. Langton's interest, and a respect for his person, that proved his strong sense of the benefits he had received. But he unfortunately fell into certain youthful indiscretions, which, if not entirely pardonable, might have been palliated by many considerations that would have occurred to a merciful man. Mr. Langton's justice, however, was seldom tempered by mercy; and, on this occasion, he shut the door of repentance against his erring *protégé*, and left him in a situation not less desperate than that from which he had relieved him. The goodness and the nobleness, of which his heart was not destitute, turned, from that time, wholly to evil; and he became irrecoverably ruined and irreclaimably depraved. His wandering life had led him, shortly before the period of this tale, to his native country. Here the erroneous intelligence of Mr. Langton's death had reached him, and suggested the scheme, which circumstances seemed to render practicable, but the fatal termination of which has been related.

The body was buried where it had fallen, close by the huge, gray, moss-grown fragment of rock,—a monument on which centuries can work little change. The eighty years that have elapsed since the death of the widow's son have, however, been sufficient to obliterate an inscription, which some one was at the pains to cut in the smooth surface of the stone. Traces of letters are still discernible; but the writer's many efforts could never discover a connected meaning. The grave, also, is overgrown with fern-bushes, and sunk to a level with the surrounding soil. But the legend, though my version of it may be forgotten, will long be traditionary in that lonely spot, and give to the rock and the precipice and the fountain an interest thrilling to the bosom of the romantic wanderer.

CHAPTER X

"Sitting then in shelter shady,
To observe and mark his mone.
Suddenly I saw a lady
Hasting to him all alone,
Clad in maiden-white and green,
Whom I judged the Forest Queen."

THE WOODMAN'S BEAR.

DURING several weeks succeeding her danger and deliverance, Ellen Langton was confined to her chamber by illness, resulting from the agitation she had endured. Her father embraced the earliest opportunity to express his deep gratitude to Fanshawe for the inestimable service he had rendered, and to intimate a desire to requite it to the utmost of his power. He had understood that the student's circumstances were not prosperous, and, with the feeling of one who was habituated to give and receive a *quid pro quo* he would have rejoiced to share his abundance with the deliverer of his daughter. But Fanshawe's flushed brow and haughty eye, when he perceived the thought that was stirring in Mr. Langton's mind, sufficiently proved to the discerning merchant that money was not, in the present instance, a circulating medium. His penetration, in fact, very soon informed him of the motives by which the young man had been actuated in risking his life for Ellen Langton; but he made no allusion to the subject, concealing his intentions, if any he had, in his own bosom.

During Ellen's illness, Edward Walcott had manifested the deepest anxiety respecting her: he had wandered around and within the house, like a restless ghost, informing himself of the slightest fluctuation in her health, and thereby graduating his happiness or misery. He was at length informed that her convalescence had so far progressed, that, on the succeeding day, she would venture below. From that time Edward's visits to Dr. Melmoth's mansion were relinquished. His cheek grew pale and his eye lost its merry light; but he resolutely kept himself a banished man. Multifarious were the conjectures to which this course of conduct gave rise; but Ellen understood and approved his motives. The maiden must have been far more blind than ever woman was in such a matter, if the late events had not convinced her of Fanshawe's devoted attachment; and she saw that Edward Walcott, feeling the superior, the irresistible strength of his rival's claim, had retired from the field. Fanshawe, however, discovered no intention to pursue his advantage. He paid her no voluntary visit, and even declined an invitation to tea, with which Mrs. Melmoth, after extensive preparations, had favored him. He seemed to have resumed all the habits of seclusion by which he was distinguished previous to his acquaintance with Ellen, except that he still took his sunset walk on the banks of the stream.

On one of these occasions, he stayed his footsteps by the old leafless oak which had witnessed Ellen's first meeting with the angler. Here he mused upon the circumstances that had resulted from that event, and upon the rights and privileges (for he was well aware of them all) which those circumstances had given him. Perhaps the loveliness of the scene and the recollections connected with it, perhaps the warm and mellow sunset, perhaps a temporary weakness in himself, had softened his feelings, and shaken the firmness of his resolution, to leave Ellen to be happy with his rival. His strong affections rose up against his reason, whispering that bliss—on earth and in heaven, through time and eternity—might yet be his lot with her. It is impossible to conceive of the flood of momentary joy which the bare admission of such a possibility sent through his frame; and, just when the tide was highest in his heart, a soft little hand was laid upon his own, and, starting, he beheld Ellen at his side.

Her illness, since the commencement of which Fanshawe had not seen her, had wrought a considerable, but not a disadvantageous, change in her appearance. She was paler and thinner; her countenance was more intellectual, more spiritual; and a spirit did the student almost deem her, appearing so suddenly in that solitude. There was a quick vibration of the delicate blood in her cheek, yet never brightening to the glow of perfect health; a tear was glittering on each of her long, dark eyelashes; and there was a gentle tremor through all her frame, which compelled her, for a little space, to support herself against the oak. Fanshawe's first impulse was to address her in words of rapturous delight; but he checked himself, and attempted—vainly indeed—to clothe his voice in tones of calm courtesy. His remark merely expressed pleasure at her restoration to health; and Ellen's low and indistinct reply had as little relation to the feelings that agitated her.

"Yet I fear," continued Fanshawe, recovering a degree of composure, and desirous of assigning a motive (which he felt was not the true one) for Ellen's agitation,—"I fear that your walk has extended too far for your strength."

"It would have borne me farther with such a motive," she replied, still trembling,—"to express my gratitude to my preserver."

"It was needless, Ellen, it was needless; for the deed brought with it its own reward," exclaimed Fanshawe, with a vehemence that he could not repress. "It was dangerous, for"—

Here he interrupted himself, and turned his face away.

"And wherefore was it dangerous?" inquired Ellen, laying her hand gently on his arm; for he seemed about to leave her.

"Because you have a tender and generous heart, and I a weak one," he replied.

"Not so," answered she, with animation. "Yours is a heart full of strength and nobleness; and if it have a weakness"—

"You know well that it has, Ellen,—one that has swallowed up all its strength," said Fanshawe. "Was it wise, then, to tempt it thus, when, if it yield, the result must be your own misery?"

Ellen did not affect to misunderstand his meaning. On the contrary, with a noble frankness, she answered to what was implied rather than expressed.

"Do me not this wrong," she said, blushing, yet earnestly. "Can it be misery? Will it not be happiness to form the tie that shall connect you to the world? to be your guide—a humble one, it is true, but the one of your choice—to the quiet paths from which your proud and lonely thoughts have estranged you? Oh, I know that there will be happiness in such a lot, from these and a thousand other sources!"

The animation with which Ellen spoke, and, at the same time, a sense of the singular course to which her gratitude had impelled her, caused her beauty to grow brighter and more enchanting with every word. And when, as she concluded, she extended her hand to Fanshawe, to refuse it was like turning from an angel, who would have guided him to heaven. But, had he been capable of making the woman he loved a sacrifice to her own generosity, that act would have rendered him unworthy of her. Yet the struggle was a severe one ere he could reply.

"Yon have spoken generously and nobly, Ellen," he said. "I have no way to prove that I deserve your generosity, but by refusing to take advantage of it. Even if your heart were yet untouched, if no being more happily constituted than myself had made an impression there, even then, I trust, a selfish passion would not be stronger than my integrity. But now"—He would have proceeded; but the firmness which had hitherto sustained him gave way. He turned aside to hide the tears which all the pride of his nature could not restrain, and which, instead of relieving, added to his anguish. At length he resumed, "No, Ellen, we must part now and forever. Your life will be long and happy. Mine will be short, but not altogether wretched, nor shorter than if we had never met. When you hear that I am in my grave, do not imagine that you have hastened me thither. Think that you scattered bright dreams around my pathway,—an ideal happiness, that you would have sacrificed your own to realize."

He ceased; and Ellen felt that his determination was unalterable. She could not speak; but, taking his hand, she pressed it to her lips, and they saw each other no more. Mr. Langton and his daughter shortly after returned to the seaport, which, for several succeeding years, was their residence.

After Ellen's departure, Fanshawe returned to his studies with the same absorbing ardor that had formerly characterized him. His face was as seldom seen among the young and gay; the pure breeze and the blessed sunshine as seldom refreshed his pale and weary brow; and his lamp burned as constantly from the first shade of evening till the gray morning light began to dim its beams. Nor did he, as weak men will, treasure up his love in a hidden chamber of his breast. He was in reality the thoughtful and earnest student that he seemed. He had exerted the whole might of his spirit over itself, and he was a conqueror. Perhaps, indeed, a summer breeze of sad and gentle thoughts would sometimes visit him; but, in these brief memories of his love, he did not wish that it should be revived, or mourn over its event.

There were many who felt an interest in Fanshawe; but the influence of none could prevail upon him to lay aside the habits, mental and physical, by which he was bringing himself to the grave. His passage thither was consequently rapid, terminating just as he reached his twentieth year. His fellow-students erected to his memory a monument of rough-hewn granite, with a white marble slab for the inscription. This was borrowed from the grave of Nathanael Mather, whom, in his almost insane eagerness for knowledge, and in his early death, Fanshawe resembled.

The Ashes of a Hard Student
and a Good Scholar.

Many tears were shed over his grave; but the thoughtful and the wise, though turf never covered a nobler heart, could not lament that it was so soon at rest. He left a world for which he was unfit; and we trust, that, among the innumerable stars of heaven, there is one where he has found happiness.

Of the other personages of this tale,—Hugh Crombie, being exposed to no strong temptations, lived and died an honest man. Concerning Dr. Melmoth, it is unnecessary here to speak. The reader, if he have any curiosity upon the subject, is referred to his Life, which, together with several sermons and other productions of the doctor, was published by his successor in the presidency of Harley College, about the year 1768.

It was not till four years after Fanshawe's death, that Edward Walcott was united to Ellen Langton. Their future lives were uncommonly happy. Ellen's gentle, almost imperceptible, but powerful influence drew her husband away from the passions and pursuits that would have interfered with domestic felicity; and he never regretted the worldly distinction of which she thus deprived him. Theirs was a long life of calm and quiet bliss; and what matters it, that, except in these pages, they have left no name behind them?

CPSIA information can be obtained
at www.ICGtesting.com
Printed in the USA
LVHW091730120121
676308LV00006B/840